C000063102

ISLE OF HOPE

Rebecca Miller

In Loving Memory

Of

Evan Necklen

1940-2018

Isle of Hope Copyright © 2020 by Rebecca Miller.
All Rights Reserved.

All rights reserved. No part of this book may be reproduced in any form or by any electronic or mechanical means including information storage and retrieval systems, without permission in writing from the author. The only exception is by a reviewer, who may quote short excerpts in a review.

Cover photo by
Hannah Miller

This book is a work of fiction. Names, characters, places, and incidents either are products of the author's imagination or are used fictitiously. Any resemblance to actual persons, living or dead, events, or locales is entirely coincidental.

Rebecca Miller
fb.me/secretpagesnz
m.me/secretpagesnz

Thank you to the lady who inspired this book, I only glimpsed you for a moment but in my mind a story unfurled.

Thank you to my heroic husband, without whom I could not have spent my days getting this written.

Thank you to my daughters, for your patience, encouragement and for sometimes having to make your own dinner.

Thank you to my treasured friend Lee, for your ongoing support and for putting me in touch with Catherine.

Thank you to my God-given sister Michelle for your unwaning belief in me and your uplifting enthusiasm.

Thank you to the Holy Spirit, for prompting me to write this book and helping me to have the perseverance to complete it.

ROMANS 8 - THE BIBLE

NEW LIVING TRANSLATION

So now there is no condemnation for those who belong to Christ Jesus.

And because you belong to him, the power of the life-giving Spirit has freed you from the power of sin that leads to death.

The law of Moses was unable to save us because of the weakness of our sinful nature. So God did what the law could not do. He sent his own Son in a body like the bodies we sinners have. And in that body God declared an end to sin's control over us by giving his Son as a sacrifice for our sins.

He did this so that the just requirement of the law would be fully satisfied for us, who no longer follow our sinful nature but instead follow the Spirit.

Those who are dominated by the sinful nature think about sinful things, but those who are controlled by the Holy Spirit think about things that please the Spirit.

So letting your sinful nature control your mind leads to death. But letting the Spirit control your mind leads to life and peace.

For the sinful nature is always hostile to God. It never did obey God's laws, and it never will.

That's why those who are still under the control of their sinful nature can never please God.

But you are not controlled by your sinful nature. You are controlled by the Spirit if you have the Spirit of God living in you. (And remember that those who do not have the Spirit of Christ living in them do not belong to him at all.)

And Christ lives within you, so even though your body will die because of sin, the Spirit gives you life because you have been made right with God.

The Spirit of God, who raised Jesus from the dead, lives in you. And just as God raised Christ Jesus from the dead, he will give life to your mortal bodies by this same Spirit living within you.

Therefore, dear brothers and sisters, you have no obligation to do what your sinful nature urges you to do.

For if you live by its dictates, you will die. But if through the power of the Spirit you put to death the deeds of your sinful nature, you will live.

For all who are led by the Spirit of God are children of God.

So you have not received a spirit that makes you fearful slaves. Instead, you received God's Spirit when he adopted you as his own children. Now we call him, "Abba, Father."

For his Spirit joins with our spirit to affirm that we are God's children.

And since we are his children, we are his heirs. In fact, together with Christ we are heirs of God's glory. But if we are to share his glory, we must also share his suffering.

Yet what we suffer now is nothing compared to the glory he will reveal to us later.

For all creation is waiting eagerly for that future day when God will reveal who his children really are.

Against its will, all creation was subjected to God's curse. But with eager hope,

the creation looks forward to the day when it will join God's children in glorious freedom from death and decay.

For we know that all creation has been groaning as in the pains of childbirth right up to the present time.

And we believers also groan, even though we have the Holy Spirit within us as a foretaste of future glory, for we long for our bodies to be released from sin and suffering. We, too, wait with eager hope for the day when God will give us our full rights as his adopted children, including the new bodies he has promised us.

We were given this hope when we were saved. (If we already have something, we don't need to hope for it.

But if we look forward to something we don't yet have, we must wait patiently and confidently.)

And the Holy Spirit helps us in our weakness. For example, we don't know what God wants us to pray for. But the Holy Spirit prays for us with groanings that cannot be expressed in words.

And the Father who knows all hearts knows what the Spirit is saying, for the

Spirit pleads for us believers in harmony with God's own will.

And we know that God causes everything to work together for the good of those who love God and are called according to his purpose for them.

For God knew his people in advance, and he chose them to become like his Son, so that his Son would be the firstborn among many brothers and sisters.

And having chosen them, he called them to come to him. And having called them, he gave them right standing with himself. And having given them right standing, he gave them his glory.

What shall we say about such wonderful things as these? If God is for us, who can ever be against us?

Since he did not spare even his own Son but gave him up for us all, won't he also give us everything else?

Who dares accuse us whom God has chosen for his own? No one—for God himself has given us right standing with himself.

Who then will condemn us? No one—for Christ Jesus died for us and was raised to life for us, and he is sitting in the place of honor at God's right hand, pleading for us.

Can anything ever separate us from Christ's love? Does it mean he no longer loves us if we have trouble or calamity, or are persecuted, or hungry, or destitute, or in danger, or threatened with death?

(As the Scriptures say, "For your sake we are killed every day; we are being slaughtered like sheep.")

No, despite all these things, overwhelming victory is ours through Christ, who loved us.

And I am convinced that nothing can ever separate us from God's love. Neither death nor life, neither angels nor demons, neither our fears for today nor our worries about tomorrow—not even the powers of hell can separate us from God's love.

No power in the sky above or in the earth below—indeed, nothing in all creation will ever be able to separate us from the love of God that is revealed in Christ Jesus our Lord.

ISLE OF HOPE

CONTENTS

CHAPTER 1 THE TEA CUP

Fingering her mother's delicate teacup in the warm soapy water, Jiao's dark-lashed eyes swept over her perfectly landscaped garden. Her nose breathed in the scent of the newly opened orange blossom outside her kitchen window and her heart yearned for the days of her youth. In her mind, Jiao drifted back to the coastal city of Qingdao and to the day that had changed the course of her life.

21st August 1995. Jiao was nineteen and it was ten years to the day since her father had been involved in a fatal 'accident' at the docks.

Jiao knew her mother would be sad, so she decided to find something to say thank you for being a good mother to her, even providing for her education as her father had wanted.

Many of the girls in Jiao's neighbourhood had never been to school. They had either dropped out years earlier to work in their family businesses or they had stayed at home learning household skills in preparation for marriage.

Jiao's Father, Mr Jianxiang Peng, had believed education was important for all and rounded the character. He had spent long hours teaching her mother to read and he had been proud of how quickly Jiao learnt and remembered new things.

On graduation from High School, Jiao had started to work full time in the little bakery around the corner from their home. It was full of flour dust, heat, steam and sweat. Usually, Jiao would hurry home to wash and change. On this day, however, Jiao had brought a change of clothes with her and on finishing work, walked the few blocks, pay packet in hand, to the large fronted, Sunny Day Department Store.

Jiao had never been inside this exclusive store before and walked in a daze looking at the opulent decor and twinkling chandeliers hanging above her. It was like entering a fairy tale palace with its majestic furniture, flamboyant furnishings, rich colours, golden embroidery, twinkling lights, and a thick red carpet she could feel her shoes sinking into. People brushed past her, purposefully headed this way or that, but Jiao had no idea which way to go. So, she stood in the foyer, looking around, wondering if she should go left or right, up the stairs or straight back out the door.

But then she heard him. Even before she saw him, her heart had begun to race and she had felt the heat rising in her cheeks.

He was standing at the top of the grand, curving staircase, his warm laughter wafting over the milling customers' heads. An elegant figure in his dark suit, she looked around to see who the lucky object of his gaze was, before realizing it was her! Their eyes met and her cheeks flushed red, Jiao turned away so he wouldn't see, but seconds later he was at her side, playfully asking "Where did you appear from, The Temple of the Heaven Goddess?"

It was a funny thing to say, instantly bringing to mind her father. He had been a devout Tsaoist and during every spring festival, would take her to The Temple of The Heaven Goddess. How she had savoured those spring days, the colours, the smells, the tastes but most of all, the pure joy of being in her gentle father's company.

Her mother believed it was her father's Tsaoist views that had led to his 'falling' and being crushed between the container ship and the wharf. She was adamant he had received threats before his death and would allow no talk of Tsaoism or visiting the temple again.

Now here was this handsome man standing before her, his mesmerizing eyes, brimming with vitality and promise, talking of the temple, with loud confidence! The deep tones of his expensive cologne filled her senses, leaving her giddy and his gaze made her want to wriggle under its boldness.

He took her hand as if she were a delicate princess and led her away from the furnishings, through treasure troves of sumptuous ornaments and jewellery until they came to the china department and that's where Jiao spotted the exquisite teacup.

Amongst all the gaudy colours and gold leaf, it was the pure, simple, beauty that caught her eye: fine china, white as snow but beautifully painted with lifelike green leaves and pink roses. She knew immediately that this was the perfect gift for her mother.

Chaoxiang was most impressed with her choice. "What delicate, refined taste, you have passed the test ...you are royalty indeed!" With that, he feigned a bow and begged her to give him the honour of accompanying her to the LianHuaGe Tea House. His behaviour was crazy and she felt embarrassed and self-conscious, sensing the eyes of the shop assistants furtively watching them.

Jiao had stifled a gasp when the sales assistant told her the price. Chaoxiang offered to pay for it, but she couldn't accept such large sum from a stranger, besides this was a gift from her, not a stranger.

Jiao did, however, consent to Chaoxiang and his companion Chongan, taking her to drink tea at the LianHuaGe Tea House. She was suddenly exceptionally thirsty, maybe it was the shock of having parted so recklessly with her hard-earned wages, maybe it was the strange effect this 'Prince Charming' was having on her.

Arriving at the doorway of the tea house, Jiao realised it was a building that had stirred her curiosity as a child. The old brick walls, the ornately engraved wooden panels around the door, the painted bamboo curtain, had all given it an air of mystery. To one side of the temple-like entrance was a giant teapot poised to pour into a large, bevelled alabaster bowl. Many moons ago, she vaguely remembered, standing with her hand in her Father's, watching water trickling out of the black pot and sparrows bathing playfully in the bowl. Out of all the coffee or tea shops, this was the one Jiao had dreamed of entering.

Through the curtain, they left the bustling city behind and Jiao found herself in a tranquil, oasis. Gentle, traditional music intermingled with the scent of earthy tea, wafted between the trees that grew inside. There was even a rock garden with gurgling brook running between the rocks. They were guided past these natural wonders, past people amicably talking and sipping around antique tables; past ornate furnishings finally ascending some old wooden steps to a small balcony. The balcony overlooked the wonderland below, but they were ushered on, into a comfortably furnished alcove which Chaoxiang obviously frequented.

Once the tea and red bean buns were served, they soon relaxed into easy conversation. From such different paths in life, it was amazing how much they found to talk about. She discovered that his Father was, in fact, the owner of the Sunny Day department store but like herself, Chao was widely read and wanted a different future for himself. They both dreamed of travelling to other lands and even liked the same classical poets.

They were not alone, Chongan, Chao's quiet, amiable friend, accompanied them, but once she had grown accustomed to the rich beauty of her surroundings, it was as though everything else melted away and it had felt to Jiao like they were the only two people in the room.

After a blissful hour of chatter and laughter, it was with regret that she looked at her wristwatch and knew it was time to leave.

The sun was going down as they walked away from the other-worldly tea house, under the trees, sprouting with spring blossoms. Chao and Chongan walked a little way with her, but then she bid them a hasty goodbye and looped back to the small rooms she shared with her Mother, down an alley off ZhongShan Road.

Arriving home, out of breath, she found her Mother still busy on her machine, working her way, as usual, through the latest pile of mending. All those years she had supported them, taking in mending along with skilfully embroidering silk and cotton tablecloths to order. Often, she had worked day and night to complete a consignment for a wealthy patron. Her handiwork was well known throughout the city. High-class ladies would seek her out; her beautiful designs had graced the tables of many a fine home and the most lavish of wedding banquets but still, she had barely scraped together a living.

Wenling had begun to suffer from arthritis in her hands and Jiao could see the pain behind her eyes as her fingers pressed down, guiding the material under the needle.

Jiao had planned to keep her unexpected rendezvous a secret, but Wenling knew instantly, that something had happened to her daughter. She saw her flushed face, the knowing smile that flickered at the corners of her mouth, dimpling her cheeks and she wouldn't stop pestering Jiao, until she'd heard the full story.

Wenling warned her to be wary, told her that rich boys treated pretty girls like her as playthings. Jiao listened to her Mother and much as she had loved Chaoxiang's sweet company, she decided that if they ever met again, she wouldn't be such easy prey.

Chaoxiang however, had known from the first moment that Jiao was the one for him.

The next day he was waiting outside the bakery where she was working, holding a lavish bouquet of red roses in the shape of a love heart, much to Jiao's embarrassed dismay.

In the weeks that followed, Chao was relentless in his pursuit of her and despite all her efforts to resist, she soon found herself falling hopelessly in love with him.

Jiao was sure that once she took him home and he saw the conditions in which she and Wenling lived, his love would waiver. So, one stormy day, with heavy heart, she invited him to her home. But, at the end of his visit, instead of rejecting her, right there, in the grimy alleyway, Chaoxiang got down on his knee and proposed marriage.

CHAPTER 2 THE HONEYMOON YEARS

They had been married within a year. Chaoxiang's Mother, Guang, was greatly opposed to the match, but his Father had accepted Jiao kindly.

To his Mother's dismay, their family Matchmaker on divining their birthdays and names had said that their marriage would be most auspicious. Jiao wondered if money had changed hands before this verdict. Chaoxiang was after all, always good at making sure that he got his own way.

He sent her many wedding gifts, including exquisite dresses in bright coloured silks and satins with the most beautiful embroidery and embellishments. Later she'd found out, his Mother had been loath to part with the family heirlooms to the likes of Jiao, so Chaoxiang had gone to his Father's store and purchased them all himself.

He had chosen the finest of all he could find; jewels and silk slippers to match every outfit, silver and gold jewellery, ornaments, expensive wine and oranges. He also sent the bride price...red envelopes full of money, more money than Jiao and her mother had ever seen. The endless deliveries began to cover every surface of their meagre dwelling, transforming their home into an Aladdin's cave.

At first, Jiao had been angry, but Chaoxiang had taken her in his arms and said it didn't matter that she didn't have a dowry, it was her he wanted and he had the means to keep her like the princess she was.

So, Jiao gave him the envelopes her father had begun to fill even when she was only eight. Every payday he had put one coin in towards this day. Wenling and Jiao had never had enough to add anything, but however much their stomachs had growled some nights, they had safely kept the envelopes untouched and hidden under the loose floorboards.

They weighed nothing next to Chaoxiang's offering to her, yet he kissed them with tears in his eyes and said, "This is your Father's blessing Jiao, I can feel him smiling down on us." He always knew how to tear at her heartstrings! At that moment, the room felt aglow and she knew that her father would have loved Chaoxiang.

Wenling, whose arthritis was worsening gave up their rented rooms and moved in with her sister in Jimo. It was from her Aunties house that Chaoxiang collected her on her wedding day, Wenling, in the absence of her Father, placed the red veil over her head. It was a wrench to say goodbye but a joy to be married to such a handsome and loving husband and to no longer be a burden on her dear Mother.

Jiao moved into her husband's family home. It was spacious enough, a large villa in the exclusive BaDaGuan district but under her mother-in-law's ever-watchful eye, Jiao felt stifled.

Chaoxiang's Mother believed he'd married beneath himself, below his station. "Of all the eligible girls in the district", she regularly chastised him, knowing Jiao was within earshot, "you chose a waif from ZhongShan Road!"

In Mrs Wang's eyes, she could do nothing right and the hours that Chaoxiang spent out doing his business, seemed endless. Sometimes, to escape the relentless chiding she wandered all day in ZhongShan Park. When she got tired, she would read under the orange blossom trees; never imagining that one day she would have gardens and orange blossom trees of her own.

Chaoxiang's father Mr Wang, owner of Sunny Day Department Store was well respected in Qingdao. He was ruggedly handsome like her husband and had the same sparkle in his eyes. Having risen to prosperity from a poor family himself, he hadn't judged Jiao on her lowly start to life but rather on her wits and intelligence. When he was there, he would defend her with a grunt and a look in Mrs Wang's direction which obviously meant 'Enough!' Mr Wang, however, being such a prominent business owner, was rarely at home.

Chaoxiang's Mother had insisted Jiao leave her job at the bakery on ZhongShan Road, saying "no daughter-in-law of hers would be seen working like a peasant." Jiao hadn't been too disappointed as it had been an early start. She did miss her independence though, the many customers she'd come to know and the satisfaction of receiving a pay-packet at the end of each week.

As it was, married life came with its own joys and demands. When they weren't trying to fulfil the family's wishes and conceive a son, Chaoxiang would keep her awake talking about his latest business ventures and the characters he had met in the city that day. She loved to listen to his deep musical voice and let her imagination follow his adventures.

Sometimes he would burst in the door and whisk her off just before dinner was due to be served, much to his Mother's dismay. Then she would get to have real-life adventures. He would hold her on his arm like royalty, introducing her to the most prominent people at business dinners in lavish hotels and restaurants.

He always wanted to know her opinion of people; he said he trusted her intuition and whenever he was in a dilemma, he wanted to know what she would do. How they would laugh after some of those nights. He would imitate his well-to-do associates until her stomach ached and she cried for him to stop.

How keen he was to get her into their chambers and out of her perfectly fitted gowns. Much to her horror, he would kiss her feet as he removed her slippers, smothering her with kisses as he unlaced her dress. How their passion used to burn through the nights. Sometimes the morning light would be seeping through the drapes before their desire was finally sated.

Soon she was with child. Chaoxiang didn't even care if it was a boy or a girl, unlike his mother, who had been forcefully advising her which months she should be having intercourse in order to conceive a boy.

Chaoxiang wouldn't even take her to find out. "If it's a boy, he will be as handsome and charming and as clever as his Dad." he would say; "If it's a girl she will be beautiful, enchanting and even cleverer, like her Mum!" His eyes would dance and he would lift her skirt to kiss her belly.

But her days had dragged. Jiao would find herself sitting at their bedroom window reading the hours away, all the time listening for the loud purr of Chaoxiang's BMW coming up the drive.

With her Mother-in law's constant instruction on what she should and shouldn't eat, how she should rest, keep her feet up and not walk too far she had been driven almost to distraction. "Eat more red beans. Don't eat that orange! Put on your slippers! Don't walk barefoot! Stop rubbing your belly!" You must do this; you mustn't do that... Jiao longed for them to escape to a place of their own.

CHAPTER 3 THEN THERE WERE FOUR

Junjie came into the world one cool autumn evening, exactly on the date he was due with little fuss and no complications.

Guang Wang hired a young girl, Lien, to be Jiao's special helper for the first few months. She was a sweet girl with a mischievous streak and a sense of humour and had helped break the monotony of Jiao's forty-day confinement.

After that, there was a grand celebration and visitations from every relative near and far. Mrs Wang was so proud of her grandson; at times Jiao felt empty-handed and dejected, waiting for her to finally grow tired of showing him off to all their visitors. Even as a baby, Junjie had his Father's distinguished features along with Jiao's striking green eyes and quickly won everyone's hearts.

Junjie hardly ever cried, and her Mother-in-Law would regularly boast that he was truly blessed by the gods. Whenever his grandmother took him in her arms, his eyes would grow wide; probably shocked by her brightly coloured clothes and heavy make-up but this just endeared him to her even more.

As he started to grow, he lived up to the meaning of his name; 'handsome and outstanding', popular with the girls and ladies and excelling in whatever he put his mind to.

When Junjie was still a toddler, Jiao found herself with child again. Chaoxiang was overjoyed and so was Jiao, especially when one balmy evening in the amber lantern light of their room, he announced that it was time they moved to a place of their own.

Jiao was very pleased when Chao took her to view a spacious apartment looking out over Fushan Bay. It belonged to family friends who were overseas and Chaoxiang thought it would be perfect for their small but growing family.

Guang Wang lamented loudly, insisting they wait until the new baby's arrival. Jiao hadn't argued too much as she was tired and appreciated the help her Mother-in-law and the house staff gave her with lively little Junjie.

Chaoxiang would bring her gifts for their new apartment and even took her to his Father's store a couple of times to choose items herself. So, the pregnancy had passed more quickly this time, with Jiao napping often, while Guang made the most of spoiling her young grandson.

As soon as Lihwa was born and Jiao was let out of the private hospital, she had insisted on moving into their beautiful apartment, now complete with furniture. Amidst ongoing protests from Guang Wang, she had packed their things and along with Lien once again employed as her helper, they had finally moved into to their own space.

She remembered dancing around the 18th storey apartment, clutching Lihwa to her breast and spinning wildly. Unlike Junjie, Lihwa had cried incessantly; only happy when upright and being jiggled in someone's arms.

How thankful Jiao was to be out from under her in-laws' roof; at least she wasn't subject to Mrs Wang's shaking head and reproach for bringing out a 'cursed child'.

Lihwa wasn't cursed, she was beautiful, with Chaoxiang's deep brown eyes, only in the wide shape of her mother's, her small, puckered lips like a pink rosebud and the softest sweetest smelling pale skin.

Chaoxiang's heart had been stolen, the moment he saw her, and he was the one who had chosen her name, 'Lihwa', meaning Princess. Although Guang visited whenever she could and every Sunday, they would spend the day at the family home. Thankfully, Mrs Wang didn't drive and so most of the week Jiao luxuriated in having her babies and her husband all to herself.

She made her own schedule, enjoying long, rambling walks in the park, taking Junjie to kindergarten some days and joining a Mother and Baby music class, where she made new friends. She met her friends for coffee, took the children to Music square or to listen to the tinkling of the sailing boats in the harbour.

Her world had opened like a flower. Chaoxiang loved returning home each evening to find her singing happily or bursting to tell him of their day's escapades. He had hugged them and swung the children in his arms, laughing at the funny things they would say.

How passionate those nights had been. In the summertime, they would open the sliding glass doors of their bedroom and make love to the rhythmic refrains of the ocean.

Standing at the sink now, Jiao remembered how her youthful and ardent husband, used to creep up behind her, to the giggles of the children, fondling her and kissing her neck while she tried to finish the dishes.

Now everything had changed. Once he had rushed home as fast as he could, at times even making up an excuse to escape a sluggish meeting, now he didn't come home at all.

She remembered him sitting patiently teaching Lihwa to form her letters, listening with a smile to her endless recounting of an event in her day that had amused her childish mind; now he couldn't even make one netball game! When had it changed?

Jiao left the kitchen and wandered into their large open plan lounge, looking out on one side over their large deck and sweeping lawns.

She sat on the new designer suite, running her fingers over the soft velvety cerise fabric, admiring the raised design that looked like black lotus flowers. She leaned back on a black silk cushion and Gengi, her little golden Maltese poodle, taking her sitting as a signal, jumped up and nestled in her lap. "At least you're still my friend, Gengi!" she said, chortling to herself.

CHAPTER 4 IMMIGRANTS

Jiao thought back to the day they had left; what a crowd had gathered at Qingdao Airport to see them off. How Mrs Chang had wailed, taking their leaving as a personal affront. "How can you do this to me?" she'd sobbed over the din of the noisy terminal.

Mr Chang, never quick to show affection, had let a tear escape his eye as he had given each of them, in turn, a long hug. Poor Lien was heartbroken, clinging first to Lihwa who was just five, then to Junjie, aged eight, then to Jiao.

Lien had become like the sister Jiao had never had and was a second mother to the children. Jiao had wished she could take her with them to this strange new land, but it wouldn't be fair. Lien had a beau and a family of her own, too much to ask her to leave behind.

Jiao had been nervous, but mostly excited. Since a girl, she had loved to read. She had especially enjoyed books about travel and adventure. The day they left she felt like she was stepping into one of her storybooks. She couldn't believe that it was happening to her! Her heart missed a beat as she stepped into the belly of the enormous, mechanical bird which would fly her to a new world, far away from everything she had ever known.

Maybe her heart wouldn't have been so light if Chaoxiang hadn't agreed to Jiao's mother, Wenling accompanying them. She remembered the sight of Wenling and Lihwa, hand in hand, Lihwa, skipping merrily and Junjie, all of eight years, standing proud beside his Father, commandeering the trolleys. At that moment Jiao had known that everything most precious to her, would be with her still.

Seventeen and a half hours later, with nearly 10,000 kilometres travelled; New Zealand wasn't as green as the pictures she'd seen. It was much busier than she expected, though the factories; houses and shops had seemed small compared to the ones in Qingdao.

Chaoxiang explained they were driving across the city of Auckland, known as 'The City of Sails'. Although a tenth of the size of Qingdao, it had about one and a half million people living there, a third of the population of New Zealand.

He told her they would drive across the Harbour Bridge and get a wonderful view of the city across the water before arriving at their apartment close to the sea. The rest of the country, he had assured her, was very green and there were mountains too, as there were in Shandong.

Chaoxiang had been travelling back and forth for three years before they had left. He had established a thriving business, importing Chinese beer into New Zealand. Having secured orders from the two large supermarket chains, he had put his good, dependable friend Chongan in charge of the Qingdao end of the business and decided he wanted to be on the ground in New Zealand. He said there would be more freedom and opportunity for the children too and they wouldn't always be looking over their shoulders and minding what they said in public for fear of being reported or detained.

At first, it had been hard for the children, going to an English-speaking school. Lihwa, just five, though shy, had gradually made Chinese and Kiwi friends and was soon speaking English fluently, often coming home with a new word or phrase to teach her mother. For Junjie it was harder, he was used to being popular and respected at school. In BaDaGuan everyone had known the Wang family, in New

Zealand, he was a 'nobody', just a new boy from a foreign land.

He'd struggled with the language despite having been learning English at school for three years. In China, Chaoxiang had paid an American to give him extra tuition but arriving in New Zealand he'd found the accent difficult to understand.

The boys his age already had friends and excluded him from their games. However, despite the shaky start, Junjie found his feet, excelling at sports as well as academics and it wasn't long before he'd won the esteem and friendship of his classmates.

Jiao had learnt to drive. Chaoxiang had insisted she should have lessons. She'd nearly given up after the first three lessons as the combination of terror at being in charge of a vehicle on the busy Auckland streets and not being able to remember anything her instructor said, had left her in despair.

Thankfully, while taking out the recycling, Wenling had been making friends with their neighbours, Mr and Mrs Chan, who had also emigrated from China. Weng Li Chan, the husband of the retired couple, had offered to give Jiao some extra lessons in the evening when it was quiet.

Every evening after seven, when the streets of Takapuna where they had lived were nearly deserted, Weng Li would sit beside Jiao gently prompting her as she turned out the gates and followed the road down to the seafront, along the beach, up again to the shops, down the empty shopping street, then around the mini-roundabout, and back down the road past their gate.

Round and round she would drive and on the fifth night Mr Chan said, "Okay, you've got that, tonight we'll drive the other way." So, she turned right out the gate and started with the roundabout. By the time her fourth lesson arrived, her confidence and driving skills had much improved and feeling less nervous, she had been able to follow her instructor's commands.

Now she couldn't imagine not being able to drive. They were a three-car family, not unusual in Auckland and quite essential since moving to a new house in an outer suburb. The tree-lined driveway and tranquil surrounds were very agreeable but to get anywhere: into the city, out of Auckland, to the airport or to a netball match, the car was an essential commodity.

Lihwa loved the fact that they lived so close to Rainbow's End, Auckland's only Theme Park. Whenever they had a free day, Lihwa and her friends would be asking for a ride there.

Soon Chaoxiang would be buying Lihwa a car for her sixteenth birthday. Was she ready to learn to drive? Junjie had learnt in weeks, the first of his friends to graduate from his Learners to a restricted licence but like his father, he always seemed worldly-wise and self-confident and no one was surprised. Lihwa was less aware of the world around her, swept along with friends, netball and her desire to be top of the class in every subject. Maybe she would excel at driving too, Jiao hoped so.

Wenling's bedroom door creaked and she hobbled down the corridor looking tired and old. She leaned on her stick as she walked painfully to the lazy boy chair across from Jiao, carefully lowering herself into it. They were having a cool, wet spring and the damp and chill in the air were setting off her arthritis again, she had suffered a lot through the winter and needed some sun to warm her aching bones.

Her mother smiled at her, but the pain prevented it from reaching her eyes. "Morning Sweetheart," she said. "I missed Lihwa again. Didn't sleep well, but at least the sun is shining today."

Jiao's heart sank, she had lost her husband; he now found his joy in reading his bankroll or in the arms of his latest young 'personal assistant'. She'd lost Junjie, loving and dutiful a son as he was; she couldn't remember the last time they had spoken heart to heart. Even when home from University for the holidays, he treated their home like a hotel, rarely there, except when sleeping or entertaining friends. Lihwa was in her own little world and had been for some years now. It was common among teenagers, but it didn't make it easier for a Mother who felt she had lost her only daughter to the world of 'self'. Then here was Wenling, her own loving Mum, her sweet soul mate, slipping away in front of her eyes, being hijacked by her pain.

Jiao let out a heavy sigh and pressed the button on the television remote. The new 75-inch TV burst into colour and sound. Chaoxiang had had it delivered a couple of weeks ago, then turned up a few nights later, all upbeat, expecting her to be grateful for it and to overlook the fact he'd not been home for over a week. Jiao had thought it too big and ostentatious, had been quite happy with their 50 inch one, but Lihwa was obviously impressed, promptly inviting her friends over for a 'Movie Night' and even Wenling seemed to like it, saying it was like being transported into other worlds. Well right now, Jiao needed transporting.

CHAPTER 5 JIAO'S IDEA

Jiao lay across the length of her super comfy sofa and flipped her hair back over the arm, as she had a habit of doing. On hot summer days, it cooled her neck, but today a cool breeze was blowing through the kitchen window; eclipsing any warmth the sun was trying to bestow. Like an ominous presence, it filled the large recesses of their home, sending a shiver down her spine.

Jiao had always thought their two-storey, six-bedroomed home, was bigger than they needed. Chaoxiang had been so excited when he had burst into their Takapuna apartment with the plans. He had bought the new property from a friend whom, halfway through constructing it for himself and his extended family, had had some bad luck in the casino. Jiao didn't know if it had been bad luck playing against her husband or if he had just turned to Chao for help. Either way, they had ended up with the deeds to an extensive house and grounds in Manakau, right on the opposite side of the city to the central beachside suburb of Takapuna, where she had just begun to feel at home.

She had got to know the faces coming and going from the apartments in their complex and they would nod or smile when they crossed paths. Even the local shop keepers in Takapuna had become friendly and familiar, asking how Jiao was or commenting about the weather. Their neighbour, Weng Li Chan, was like a Father to her. He had lost his only daughter when she was 21; she would have been the same age as Jiao. He often looked at her with a special affection that told her he was thinking of his daughter.

Mrs Chan was quiet and kind, she and Wenling loved to sit on the balcony and look out over the ocean. Often, they would sit in comfortable silence, other times they would share stories and laughter, reminiscing about their youthful days in homeland China. Knowing that her Mum was content, Jiao was able to go for walks on the wide sandy beach and loved the feeling of freedom she felt when the salty wind blew through her hair and the waves lapped over her bare feet.

It was hard to leave this newly made life, especially for such isolation. Initially, on visiting the building site with Chaoxiang, she had tried to hide her dismay and had looked away when tears escaped her eyes. The first floor had been constructed and the grandiose teardrop-shaped driveway with the covered porch was freshly dried concrete. While she could appreciate the elegant and practical design, it looked more like a hotel than a home. It was located off a fast field and fence edged road with a long private driveway down to their property and the thought of her nearest neighbour being so far away, made her heart sink.

She had suggested renting it out. "We could use it as another income stream." But Chaoxiang had laughed his hearty laugh and putting his arm around her, whispered in her ear, "We have plenty of money in the bank, my love, don't worry your pretty head about that, you can use your good sense of taste to choose the decoration!"

She had even raised the idea of getting some boarders. Chao had irritably poo-pooed that idea too, saying "I'm not having strangers living in my house!"

So, Jiao had stopped her protests and busied herself choosing the flooring, paint and finishes and finally furniture and furnishings until the day came to say goodbye to their safe apartment and the sound of the sea and to arrive at their lonely, whitewashed mansion.

The rain had been unrelenting, the day they moved in. Jiao felt like the sky was crying; just like she was inside. Nothing dampened Chaoxiang's pleasure though as he directed the removal men to deposit their belongings into the correct rooms. He always loved being in charge and felt proud to have outdone his parent's villa in BaDaGuan, even though they weren't there to see it.

Chao took great joy in endowing Jiao with more than she needed but he seemed oblivious to her sorrow. Wenling was heartbroken too at leaving the Chans, but she understood the pride Chao took in providing for them so lavishly. He had told Wenling that she could call his private driver anytime and he would take her back for visits, but Jiao knew her Mum would never dream of 'imposing' on Chaoxiang.

Having successfully commandeered the Chinese beer market in New Zealand, Chao had now made a new partnership with an old friend from University. He was making his fortune buying and selling gold in Shandong and Chao was to open trading channels in New Zealand. He was enjoying this new challenge, expanding his business circles and spending more and more time 'at the office'.

So, Jiao had found herself increasingly alone in the modern expanse of her new home, with only her mother to talk to as she'd struggled to resettle the children into new schools. What made it worse was that Liwha had still been at primary school while Junjie was starting Intermediate school, so they hadn't even had each other for support. This time, the situation had reversed, Junjie had made friends quickly but Liwha had struggled, crying herself to sleep each night, arising pale and shaky each morning.

It had broken Jiao's heart to see her daughter so unhappy and she'd begun to feel angry at Chao for causing them all so much pain, for not realising he had and most of all, for not being there to help them through it.

She had thrown herself into the garden, employing landscape gardeners and researching plants and flowers. With half a hectare of land to beautify, it had been a pleasant distraction when the children were at school.

On sunny days Wenling would follow her out with her folding chair and talk to her as she worked. Nowadays she rarely ventured further than the large wooden deck Jiao had constructed outside the lounge room. She'd incorporated sunken planters, coloured lights and especially for her Mum, who loved birds, a water feature with a birdbath at the bottom. She'd planted some natives to attract a menagerie of local species and Wenling loved to watch them and listen to their strange songs. "Even the birds sing in different languages here!" she would laugh. She especially loved the black and white tuis with their crested heads and low repetitive calls, the screechy fantails, and the green parakeets with their colourful heads that looked like they'd escaped from a cage.

The lawn fell away in a sweeping slope, with views to the different gardens Jiao had established: the rose garden; the rockery; the herb garden; the tropical walk and the sculpture garden.

There was also the tennis court Chaoxiang had wanted, to improve his fitness, but although it was initially popular with the children and their friends, sending lovely peals of laughter floating over the lawn to the deck, now it sat unused gathering leaves. He should have built a netball court she thought to herself, then at least Liwha would use it and she might see a bit more of her daughter.

Jiao let out a deep sigh, thinking back on all these things. One day when Chaoxiang hadn't been home for two weeks, (he'd been at his suite in the Sky City Grand Hotel, from where he liked to conduct his meetings and entertain his prospective business associates) she had told him how lonely she was feeling. He had been distracted, obviously in the middle of an important deal and she hadn't thought he had heard her.

The next week, however, a delivery had arrived. On the doorstep stood a gentleman in white, holding a strange looking box pierced with holes. He set it down inside the doorway, returning to his minivan for another box. Cautiously opening the strange-smelling box, she had discovered a scared little ball of golden fluff and curls, looking up at her with round pool-like eyes and a black button nose. "A Maltese Poodle," the man had announced with satisfaction, "otherwise known as a 'Maltipoo'". Jiao was instantly smitten with love for the vulnerable looking pup.

The friendly old man, who had driven all the way from a pet shop in Takapuna, proceeded to unpack the other large cardboard box, explaining the contents. "Wet food; dry food; bed; bedding; toys; a soft bristle brush ... don't forget to brush him every day!; nail clippers; vaccination records; tablets; a toothbrush; doggie toothpaste; dog shampoo; a variety of collars, leads and coats and fresh breath treats." Someone had thought of everything, Jiao wondered if it was Chaoxiang's beautiful, new, personal assistant; he had mentioned she lived in Takapuna. Jiao had pushed the thought from her mind and thanked the shopkeeper.

She smiled at the thought of the joy that the little creature had brought to the home. They had named him 'Gengi' meaning 'Gold' due to his soft golden coat. It seemed ironic to Jiao that it was Chaoxiang's pre-occupation with the stuff that had led to her needing a companion. It was a bit sad really that her husband had bought her a dog for company rather than spending time with her himself.

Gengi had brought new life into the home, for that she was thankful. Both the children began to laugh and play more, running around the house and garden. Jiao and Wenling would laugh until tears ran down their cheeks watching Junjie chase the little pup down the lawn until Gengi would suddenly turn about and chase Junjie yelling as if his life were at stake, back up the grassy slope. At night, Liwha could often be found hugging Gengi to her chest, sharing all her troubles with her newfound friend.

Gengi was friendly and sociable with everyone, always wanting to be in the middle of whatever was happening, but most of all, he doted on Jiao and his adoring eyes followed her every move. She loved having him beside her as she weeded the garden, even if he did try and help by digging up the flowers.

She had begun with the resolute announcement that Gengi would sleep in his own bed in the lounge, not in the bedrooms. But he had cried whenever Jiao closed her door and gradually, she had caved in. At first, she had moved his bed in her room, but he had still cried quietly. Then she had conceded to him laying his head on her feet, gazing lovingly at her until his eyes closed, finally peaceful nights had resumed! Still, Jiao missed her husband and wished that he were as desperate for her company as Gengi was and longed to see his eyes filled with as much love.

As if sensing her thoughts, Gengi nuzzled in a little closer. Jiao glanced over at her Mum, about to offer her some tea, but saw her eyelids lightly fluttering as she took forty winks. The AM show had been interrupted yet again by commercials.

When they had first arrived, there had only been one Chinese channel on TV, Jiao had gravitated to it, enjoying listening to her Mother tongue being spoken. But Chaoxiang had scolded her saying, "How do you expect your children to integrate into New Zealand society when all they see and hear at home is Chinese language and culture?" She had understood the point he'd made and began to watch English TV, particularly current affairs and local programmes. She had hoped this would give her some interesting topics to discuss with her husband too. But as he had come home less and less often, it ended up being Mrs Chan and Wenling she'd had those discussions with.

They also watched 'Shortland Street' a New Zealand soap opera set in a Hospital in Auckland. Like most of the Chinese television dramas, it was very melodramatic and Jiao and Wenling used to joke that they hoped they never got admitted to a hospital that was like that, with its regular murders and love triangles!

Wenling snored quietly in her chair, catching up on some of the sleep that had eluded her during the night. Looking up at the crystal-clear screen, Jiao saw turquoise waters lapping the sandy white beaches of Rarotonga and she had an idea.

CHAPTER 6 JIAO'S ADVENTURE BEGINS

Jiao's skin crawled with fear and excitement. The day had come. Chao hadn't made any objection or suggested coming with her and Liwha thought it was a sweet idea for Mom and 'Lao Lao' as she called her Grandmother, to have a holiday together. Junjie, who was at Uni and had been pre-occupied with planning his own summer trip to Thailand had told her to "Have fun and don't do anything I wouldn't!". Jiao had arranged for Mrs Chan to mind the house and Liwha while they were away.

Mrs Chan's husband, Weng Li, had died peacefully in his sleep two years earlier, so Lifen Chan now lived alone. Jiao and Wenling would often invite her to stay for a few days as they worried about her being lonely. She even had her own room reserved especially for her visits.

Liwha loved talking to Mrs Chan whose Father had been a Lawyer and before she married, had worked as a legal secretary for her Father's law firm. Lihwa whose heart was set on becoming a lawyer would bombard Lifen with questions whenever she had the chance. Despite her years, Lifen's mind was surprisingly lively. She still loved to follow court cases, politics and to read extensively. She was a quiet and peaceful person but also a font of knowledge on many subjects. Lihwa rarely came out of her room. She always had her head in her books or in her laptop, except when she was playing netball, so Jiao felt happy to leave her daughter with Lifen, knowing she wouldn't be able to resist talking to her! Fred, her gardener would be working most days too, so she didn't need to worry about the garden or Lifen not having enough company.

Fred had appeared one day, in his little green truck, announcing that a neighbour had sent him and did she need some help. Jiao never did find out which neighbour had sent him, but in the middle of digging out roots to create a rose garden, she had certainly appreciated his help that day and every week for the seven years since

Fred had become a part of their household. Steady and reliable, he would turn up each day, always with a smile and a kindly word, often with a new joke that Jiao would sometimes have to get the children to explain to her. "I was walking down the street", he'd told her one day, "and I saw a man looking sad and lonely, so I stopped him and said, 'you should go to the café on the corner, they've got a sign in the window that says 'Free Wifee'." Junjie and Lihwa had giggled as they had explained the play on words to her. "It's Kiwi humour they'd said, you'll get it one day Mum." Jiao did get it but just not always straight away.

I wonder if Rarotongan humour is the same a Kiwi humour, she thought to herself, as she checked the contents of her case for at least the tenth time, checked her fully ticked off list one last time, then zipped it shut.

Chaoxiang had messaged to say he'd organised a car and driver to pick them up. Jiao felt disappointed that he hadn't come to say goodbye. She hadn't seen him since Sunday and then he'd only stayed for a few hours. He had smelt of someone else's perfume and been quick to have a shower and change before joining them for afternoon tea. She couldn't remember the last time they'd been intimate, and she'd felt a pang of grief and jealousy. Why did he treat her like a simple child? Maybe he **had** married beneath himself. If he had married someone from an honourable family like his own, someone university educated, someone who had travelled, maybe he would want to come home to her and not look to other women.

Jiao's ears pricked up as she thought the car had arrived, but it was just Fred's old van bumbling down the drive and stopping with a clunk at the top of the lawn. She could hear his and Lifen's mumbled voices followed by a peal of laughter. It was good to hear the sombre widow laugh. Fred was certainly magical like that.

Yesterday he'd said to her, "Why did God create man before woman?" Jiao had waited with interest expecting a theological answer; instead, he said: "Because He didn't want any advice on how to do it!"

She would miss Fred: his easy companionship; his funny humour. Jiao had found it strange at first that he would joke about a holy book. She once asked him outright if he believed in the Bible and it had stuck in her mind how his old eyes had sparkled like a child's as he nodded vehemently and said: "Oh Yes Jiao and every word of it is true, every word, it's the living truth!"

She hadn't really understood what he meant by that, but sometimes when they had been working on their knees on a patch of garden, Fred had told her amazing stories she had loved to hear. She would always ask him at the end, "Was that from the bible Fred?" "Oh Yes." He would reply, nodding his head in an all-knowing way.

Jiao especially loved the story of Esther, what twists and turns her life had taken! Her Family had been taken as slaves to a foreign land, then her parents had died, but thankfully she had been taken in by her cousin. Next, because she was beautiful and a virgin, she was taken to the King's harem; where she was given beauty treatments for a year before being presented to the King. Out of all the girls, he had chosen to make her his Queen.

Then the King's right-hand man had sent out a decree that all her people should be slaughtered. Their land and belongings were to be taken by whoever killed them. The King didn't know Esther was a Jew. Risking her life, she presented herself before him unsummoned, but thanks to her bravery and obedience to her God, her people were saved and their enemies were killed instead.

A decree was made and to this day the Jewish people celebrate Purim when they remember how God used Esther to save their people and deliver them from their enemies.

The story reminded her of the story of Princess Guan Yin. Her Father had known lots of stories. He had loved the library and sometimes they had gone together to sit for hours poring over old books and their beautiful illustrations. He had been a good storyteller too.

The story of Guan Yin had always been her favourite. Like Esther, she was outstandingly beautiful, not an orphan, but the youngest daughter. She was intelligent, compassionate and loved by all. Her Dad had wanted her to marry and be the heir to his kingdom.

Like Esther, she had heard and obeyed a higher voice, but this had put her at discord with her Father. She believed she was called to remain pure and live a quiet life; this angered the King, so she ran away. She sought refuge in a convent but was treated like a low life servant, forced to carry wood and heavy pails of water up and down the mountain.

Even when the Dragon God magically made a well appear, complete with an inscription of her name, at the top of the hill outside the convent the nuns continued to treat her with disdain. Only when her Father sent his army to burn the convent down and bring her home, did the nuns realise who she was.

She prayed and the Gods heard her, sending rain to put out the fire. Returning shamed to her Father, he prepared a feast for her and gave her another chance to marry. Though she loved him, she had to stay true to her calling and she refused. Furious he put her to death.

Arriving in the lower world of torture, such was her goodness that the kingdom of death began to burst into blossom. The King of that dominion, appalled that one of such purity and kindness should enter his bloody kingdom, sent her to Heaven where she was bestowed with immortality.

Jiao had loved that story of Guan Yin and how she had become the Goddess of Mercy. As a girl, Jiao had wished she could be good and perfect like Guan Yin, but she had always seemed to let herself down.

When her father had died, she had prayed to Guan Yin but the silence and heaviness that had filled their little home had just made her feel more alone and bereft. She sometimes wondered if her pride and selfishness had caused Tsao Shen to have her Father taken from her.

At the end of each lunar year after his death, when her mother would take down the picture of Tsao Shen, the

Kitchen God, from above their hearth, having smeared his lips with honey in the hope he would speak only kind words about them to Shanti, the god of judgement, Jiao would shake with fear. She would remember all the times she had put herself first or been less than perfect and her heart would fill with dread that her mother too would be taken from her.

Jiao smiled lovingly as she thought of her dear Mum, how she had buoyed her through all the ups and downs life had bestowed. She never cajoled or criticized, always supported her marriage to Chao, despite her initial objection to it, backed her up in all her parenting decisions and knew her heart even when she didn't say a word.

The driver had arrived; the car must have pulled in silently, but she could hear someone speaking in Mandarin to Wenling, with a soft accent Jiao couldn't quite place. She swung the giant clamshell of a case onto the floor.

She had planned to buy herself some new luggage, maybe a medium case with a matching bag. She had been to the mall and looked at some fun ones with colourful, tropical prints but then Chaoxiang had come home with this pearly, iridescent, Samsonite, 'high security' case.

It was ridged like a seashell with four swivel wheels and a vanishing, pull-along handle. Not quite what she had been planning, larger and much more ostentatious, as everything Chao bought was, but certainly it was beautiful in its own giant tropical shell kind of way! She wheeled it down the corridor and carried it carefully down the stairs.

Wenling seemed surprisingly relaxed about the new adventure. They had never been anywhere on a plane except their two-yearly visits to Qingdao. They had gone for a few days to Sydney when the children were younger and a week in Dubai for a family holiday once, but Chaoxiang had organized everything and Wenling and Jiao had just followed with the children like ducklings.

This time was completely different. Once she had been given her husband's approval, Jiao had walked into her local travel agent shop and told them what she wanted. She had returned home with a folder of brochures, information and flight details, flights and hotel booked!

Chaoxiang on seeing the tickets had insisted on calling the agent immediately and got them upgraded to business class as first wasn't available on the short-haul flight. That was four months ago, now it was the end of March, summer days drawing to an end in New Zealand, but Rarotonga would still be warm, so the travel agent had assured her.

The driver, a small-built, middle-aged man, complete with a black suit, white shirt and black cap, was loading Wenling's case into the back of a midnight black jaguar sparkling in the morning sun. Her Mother's case was bright turquoise; she had chosen it the last time they had gone back to Qingdao. Jiao had been surprised that she had chosen something so loud, but then Wenling did occasionally surprise her daughter. This trip, for example, she had expected her Mum to be resistant to the idea, homebody that she tended to be, but instead she was enthusiastic.

The smart chauffeur, chatting cheerfully, carefully helped Jiao's Mum into the back seat. He had newly arrived in Auckland and was enjoying working for Mr Wang and now serving his family. He saluted and bowed numerous times when he saw Jiao, but she couldn't help smiling back at the enormous grin that covered his face from ear to ear.

"What's your name?" she asked, trying to be serious.

"Peng Sun", he said, bowing on each syllable. "At your service," he added, bowing again before springing light-footed up the steps, to take her case and bag from her hands. She hung on to her handbag, wanting to keep their passports and travel information close at hand but let him lift her light case into the boot of the luxury sedan car.

It certainly was a beautiful car, similar to the one she'd seen the British Prime Minister being driven in, on the news last night. Chao was always one for grand gestures, this was no exception, but in her heart, Jiao wished he had wanted to spend some time with her before she left or could have come himself to say goodbye, how she longed for his embrace. She'd forgotten what it felt like to be held in his arms.

As they belted up and settled into the soft leather scented seats of the Jaguar sedan, only Lifen Chan and Fred stood on the marble steps waving them goodbye.

CHAPTER 7 KIA ORANA

Jiao needn't have been anxious, the check-in and security at Auckland International Departures had been straight forward, so much smaller than Qingdao Airport. They had even had time for a leisurely lunch in the airport departure terminal.

The four-hour flight had passed quickly. Jiao and Wenling had shared a miniature bottle of champagne and watched a newly released movie and now the plane shuddered as it made its descent. Wenling grabbed Jiao's hand for reassurance. Unlike her daughter who loved the thrill of flying, she much preferred to have her feet on solid ground. Looking out the window, Jiao could see a palm-covered island drenched in orange and gold as the sun set over it. It was like a travel agent's poster.

By the time she was helping her Mum, with her stiff joints, manoeuvre the steps of the plane, the sun had gone, and the only light was coming from the A-Frame terminal building.

As they exited the plane, the balmy warmth enveloped Jiao, reminding her of a cosy feather and down comforter. She breathed a sigh of happiness.

They fumbled their way towards the light, Jiao trying to support her mother while struggling to find her night vision. She stopped to take a photo of the illuminated writing over the doors 'Kia Orana' 'Welcome to the Cook Islands'. Wenling leaned on her case and rested; gentle ukulele music drifted over them on the humid, sweet-scented air.

Entering through the doors of the glass A-Frame airport, was like walking into a greenhouse, the empty conveyer belt moving, ready for the oncoming luggage, was surrounded by tropical plants. An old man stood propped against the wall beside it, with a flower print shirt and a straw hat fringed with bright coloured flowers. He strummed his Ukulele rhythmically, singing "Kia Orana, Kia Orana, Kia Orana" in a soft welcoming voice.

The deep floral scent of gardenia and frangipani wafted from somewhere; the terminal was abuzz with life and laughter. The Ukulele man began to play, Elvis Presley's 'Welcome to My World' bringing back memories of Mr Chan, he had a vinyl recording of it which he had loved to play on his 'retro' turntable. Lifen had even played it at his funeral. Hearing it again somehow made Jiao feel that she was not alone.

She smiled at the old man strumming and to her surprise; he looked straight in her eyes and smiled back. The island lady beside her gave her a friendly smile too. "Know Papa Jake, do you?" she asked. "Err, no." Jiao stammered. "Thirty-Five years he's been here," she said. "Never misses a flight. He's my great uncle. Used to be a firefighter here on the runway..." she pointed back through the doors where their plane still sat. "He'd jump out his fire truck and quickly change so he could welcome the passengers as they disembarked! He's retired now but still the one you can rely on to always welcome you home." She gazed lovingly at her Uncle, who must have felt her eyes on him, as he turned and gave her a warm grin.

The luggage was coming around now and Jiao tensed up, waiting to pounce when she saw her case. Wenling was sitting on a seat clinging to their hand baggage, so Jiao had her hands free. This had always been Chao's job, retrieving their cargo. One time in Qingdao Airport, someone had taken Wenling's case. Chao had had a tug of war with the shifty looking man while ordering Jiao to call the security. The awful thing was, it actually was the man's case, exactly the same as Wenling's, but it had his name written on it. Jiao chuckled to herself ... maybe that's why the next one she chose had been bright turquoise; she doubted there would be more than one of those today.

Beginning to scrutinize the luggage, Jiao was surprised to see lots of bulging flimsy bags, ones you could buy from a two-dollar shop, made of woven plastic, most secured with nothing more than a bit of brown tape. People were hauling them off the belt, double-checking their bold labels.

Then she spotted white polystyrene cool boxes, with big sticky labels: "Longo Mauariki" one said "Rakanui Family" another. Catching her puzzled expression at the sight of such strange luggage, the lady beside her, Papa Jake's niece said, "Chicken ...they're full of chicken ...us Cookies love our chicken! "...as if that explained everything. Jiao was still confused, but spotting her case followed by Wenling's in close succession, she leapt into action, hauling them off and trying to drag them both at once to where her Mum sat. Papa Jake had finished his song and looking at her called out, "There's a trolley this side over here, so you don't have to carry your bags." Jiao and a couple of other tourists made their way around the slow-moving belt and found trolleys.

Passing through customs Jiao declared her Laoshan tea; their favourite green tea from Laoshan Mountain in Qingdao. Her father had first introduced it to them after going on a pilgrimage up the mountain. It was the most fragrant tea she'd ever discovered and brewed into a clear, jade liquor had a fresh but mellow flavour. She had never forgotten that first taste or how she would open the paper bag in their kitchen larder, just to inhale the fragrance of the mountain. Her Mother had kept it for guests and special occasions. When she had told Chaoxiang the story, he had insisted on finding a source and had kept them in supply ever since.

The rotund, straight-faced customs official slowly examined the tea with almost exaggerated interest. He lifted the sealed package above his face and inhaled deeply. "Mmmm. Smells very good!" he announced finally, "Where are you staying?" 'Oh No,' thought Jiao, 'was she in trouble, did he think it was drugs?' but no sooner had she blurted out the name of their hotel, than a big island grin cracked across his face. "I'll be around for a cup of tea then!" he joked, letting out a giant island guffaw.

Jiao who had been starting to panic, more at the thought of three weeks without their favourite brew than anything else, let out a sigh of relief as he replaced it in her case and put it to one side for her to zip back up. All the time Papa Jake's joyful ukulele music was playing loudly.

Wenling had gone straight through the adjacent checkpoint and was sitting on some seats outside a mini duty-free liquor store, watching the merry mayhem around her.

The travel agent had told Jiao to look for someone holding a sign with their hotel name on, so as they went through the final checkpoint, showing their passports, she began scanning the upheld signs.

Beside her, a long-missed family member walked through the barriers into a noisy mass of bodies, all decked out in bright bold island prints and adorned with flowers, even the men. The new arrival, a slim woman, about Jiao's age, was getting squeezed in each of their open island arms, garlands of fresh flowers thrown over her head until she was only just peeping over them. They put a flower crown on her head, kissed her cheeks and touched their noses with hers; some were crying tears of joy.

What a show of affection Jiao thought, how loved that woman must feel. How different her homecoming would be. She felt a lump in her chest. It had been there before, resentment? Disappointment? She wasn't sure, but what had felt like a small gnawing, had grown and hardened.

Jiao spotted a sign with the name of their hotel in bold black pen, held up by a slightly harassed lady, in a gaudy red and mustard island print dress. Jiao manoeuvred the trolley that way. She walked slowly as her mum hung onto her arm, still stiff and painful from the flight.

The woman smiled as they reached her, a superficial smile. A stocky man appeared beside her in matching shirt, a large orange hibiscus flower sticking out from behind his ear. "Kia Orana! Welcome to Rarotonga" he announced jovially, "Name?" Jiao gave their names and he checked them off on his clipboard. When he'd done this, he took a garland of flowers from his arm and threw it over Jiao's neck. "Kia Orana," he said again then flipped another one over Wenling's head. Although there was no love and affection in the action, as there had been towards the woman Jiao had observed, the aroma of the flowers was pungent and stirred something deep in her senses.

A party of four arrived and were delivered the same greeting, checked off and garlanded too. Finally, a family with two young, obviously tired and irritable children and an elderly couple arrived. The checklist complete and everyone suitably bedecked with flowers, the woman tucked the sign under her arm and the flowery eared man, began to usher them towards a white bus, labelled 'Island Tours'.

Bags stowed and relieved to be sitting again, they pulled out the small airport carpark onto the road that encircled the Island. Jiao hoped that the hotel wasn't far away and that they weren't actually embarking on an island tour. Excited as she was at having arrived, even after such a short journey, Jiao felt physically and emotionally exhausted and hoped their new 'home' for the next few weeks would be clean and comfortable.

After just a few minutes on the bus, during which they were unable to see much but shadows of huts, trees and buildings, some lit up by colourful fairy lights, the bus swung off the main road and made its way up a palm-lined driveway. Reaching the top, it stopped beside a large brightly lit foyer. There was a seating area, a dark, solid wooden L-shaped desk to one side and to the other the building was open onto a wide path. At the desk, Jiao was given two room keys and then what looked like a golf buggy appeared on the pathway. The receptionist pointed out Jiao and Wenling and the young man driving it, jumped out and loaded their bags onto the back, before carefully helping them both aboard.

Minutes later, having passed sweet-scented trees and a couple of floodlit tennis courts, they were delivered to their room. Jiao turned the key with trepidation; after booking it she had read some mixed reviews about this hotel.

She needn't have worried; the room was clean bright and airy with frangipani pictures on the walls. There were two queen beds with white bedcovers printed with beautiful orange, yellow and pink blooms. The furniture was light bamboo, bedside tables, a substantial writing desk, a sofa and chairs with deep pink pads and pretty flowery cushions, nicely arranged around a glass-topped table. The curtains were deep fuchsia, matching the colour of the flowers on the cushions and bedcovers and on the glass table was an exotic arrangement of pink and orange anthuriums in a round glass vase.

"Everything OK Madam?" asked the young island boy who had been driving the buggy.

"Yes, everything is very good. Thank you." She pressed some money into his palm as she had learnt was good practice from her husband.

The boy's face lit up." Anything you need Madam, I 'll be happy to help." Then he quickly hopped back onto the buggy, disappearing into the darkness.

That night Jiao lay awake. A warm breeze gently blew through the curtains. Beyond the curtain the full moon bathed the calm ocean in golden light, the picture of perfection. But lying beneath the crisp cotton covers, all Jiao could hear was the thrashing of the waves beyond the tranquil waters, crashing on the reef, roaring louder and louder like a shackled lion.

CHAPTER 8 STRANGER ON THE BEACH

The next morning Jiao awoke with the dawn. Although only a slither of light infiltrated the dark womb of their room, the ocean was calling to Jiao.

Quietly she slipped on her silky aqua green dragon print robe and tiptoed past her mother's bed, sliding her hand through the curtains, she unlocked the balcony door then stole her whole self through the curtain crack.

She was greeted by a whole new world. The morning sun was setting the sky aglow and the sand below was almost bedazzling in its whiteness. The palm trees on either side of their balcony rustled in the warm breeze, whispering conspiringly to her. She was tempted to jump the balcony rails onto the soft sand below; they were on the ground floor, so it wasn't far!

Remembering her nakedness beneath her robe and thin negligée, she snuck back through the curtains, tiptoed to her case and found her new black bikini and a white maxi beach dress. After donning them quietly in the bathroom, she turned the key in the door and set herself free.

Out on the beach, her senses were hit once again with the intoxicating smell of frangipanis and gardenias. She could hear the distant peal of pots and dishes from the restaurant kitchen, where breakfast preparation was underway.

Turning away from the pretty pathway leading to the beachfront restaurant, Jiao revelled in the gentle breeze that made the silk chiffon of her dress, waft around her like an apparition. The early morning sun, already warm on her cheeks gave her a sense of wellbeing. She wondered how many days it would take before freckles reappeared on her cheeks and nose. Really, they were "Sun-kisses" according to her gardener, Fred. The sunlight, warming her cheek, almost did feel like a lingering lovers kiss.

Just as she was thinking this, Jiao saw a bronzed figure coming towards her. She squinted her eyes to see him more clearly and sure enough, it was the figure of a man, fit and tanned, his muscles firm, catching the sun's rays as he ran. Jiao wondered if the sun was kissing his muscles too, she certainly would if she could. At this thought, the blood rushed to her face and then before she knew it, he was there, standing before her.

Seeing Jiao, he had stopped in his tracks and was catching his breath. He was a young man, not much older than her son, wearing a skimpy pair of running shorts. Jiao couldn't help noticing his thick, toned thighs and his golden island skin before registering his face. He was looking at her with full recognition. "Morning Madam or should I say Kia Orana! Did you sleep well?" Jiao suddenly realised it was the bag boy! The one who had delivered them to their room and to whom she'd given the tip. He certainly looked older and very handsome in the daylight ...without his clothes. She felt herself blushing again and saw a flicker of a smile cross his lips. She suddenly felt very alive, her body was tingling, and she knew he found her attractive too. The heat between them was more than just the sun's rays.

His eyes were those of a man, not a boy and his lips broke into a full smile that she knew in her heart was genuine and kind. He cleared his throat and spoke again, his voice sounded husky, "Enjoy your day Madam, if you need anything, let me know." Then he dipped his head at her and proceeded to run back towards the hotel.

Jiao's mind was in a whirl. What was she thinking, lusting after a man probably half her age? She was married and what would Chaoxiang do if he ever found out she had been with another man? She could lose everything... her home, her family. Her Mum would be shamed. It was one thing for a man to have extramarital affairs, but a woman, no that would be shameful.

Her heart sunk in her chest, how unfair this world was... dangling happiness like a sparkling diamond before you but if you put it on, it would turn into a millstone! Just like her dreams of a happy family, of working alongside Chaoxiang, sharing the highs and lows of life, along with his bed. Maybe like Guan Yin, she should have found a convent and taken a vow of chastity; at least then she wouldn't know what she was missing. Beside her, the sea lapped at the sand, sucking it into itself. Jiao remembered their nights in Qingdao, making love to the sound of the sea thrashing the harbour wall.

Inside her yearning to love and be loved began to feel more like rage. She didn't just long to burn with passion, she wanted to be consumed. She thought of the young man, she didn't even know his name. Maybe that was better. He had ignited her desire and maybe he could relieve the ache inside her. She could arrange a secret meeting with him, maybe at night, on the beach while her Mother slept soundly. No one would ever know.

As she turned and made her way back to the hotel, she passed a couple of tourists, hand in hand, making their way to breakfast. They smiled at her but all she could see was the image of her virile island man, with his knowing smile, telling her, "Anything you need."

Arriving at their room Jiao found her Mum awake, sitting on their balcony enjoying a cup of Laoshan tea. She was smiling and it looked like the Island air was already restoring some colour into her frail, pale skin.

At breakfast, Jiao found she was surprisingly hungry and returned to the buffet several times for herself and her mother. The fresh pawpaw, chunks of firm coconut flesh, bananas and crimson dragon fruit, tasted like no fruit she had ever bought in New Zealand. The flavours were fresh and vibrant. She tried the 'Bircher Muesli' a cold runny, oat porridge, but so cooling and delicious. Then there were the warm banana muffins with their fluffy sponge and tangy banana pieces. The pineapple juice was sweet and refreshing. Finally, they rounded off their extended meal with steamy bitter coffee (and one more irresistible, melt-in-the-mouth muffin).

Happy and complete, they sat at their outdoor table, watching the dappled colours of the sea. The travel agent had mentioned that she had seen whales while eating her breakfast in the same resort, so Jiao strained her eyes for a sighting. The more she gazed at the sparkling blue of the ocean, the more shadows, fin-like shapes and random splashes of waves she saw. Each time she thought she'd spotted something, her heart would skip a beat... "Fish", "Turtle!", "Dolphin?". In the end, the game was driving her crazy, so she dragged her eyes away.

She began to look instead at the faces of the staff; they stood out from the tourists with their bright Island print dresses and shirts. The wait staff wore lime green with brown and white flowers, someone came through from reception and spoke to a guest, swapping a key with them, she was in blue and white, so she guessed that was the reception uniform. Nearby, at the activities hut, a Robinson Crusoe type construction, young men in red logoed t-shirts stood around laughing. Jiao searched the faces of the young men but didn't see her mystery man from the beach. She hadn't noticed his attire in the cover of darkness the night before, so wondered which uniform was his. She did remember the sight of him that morning though, his wide bronzed chest, skimpy shorts, strong brown thighs, her face flushed at the memory and she was thankful her Mother couldn't read her mind.

Wenling was sitting head back, eyes closed, drinking in the warmth of the Rarotongan sunshine. She wore a new short-sleeved summer dress in light jade green, with a tiny pink flamingo print. Jiao had looked closely to see what they were, smiling to herself when she'd realised, they were pink birds ...her Mum loved birds! She wore matching sandals, in the same green, but iridescent, the straps caught the sun's rays, cleverly creating shimmers of pink. She wore a necklace and earrings of small light jade beads. She had even applied some rouge and rosy pink lipstick. It was such a change to see her so full of colour, her go-to wardrobe in New Zealand was black pants and often grey pullovers or long dark cardigans. Before leaving New Zealand, Wenling had gone on an obviously bounteous shopping excursion with Lifen; Jiao looked forward to seeing what other surprises she would appear in.

Their first day passed leisurely. Returning to their room, Wenling read a book on the balcony while Jiao swam in the sea. There were some rocks, but the water was so clear that it was easy to find large sandy patches, like underwater beaches. She didn't venture very deep as her eyes were still playing tricks with her every time, she let them wander.

She saw some children throwing bread on the water then laughing and squealing as fish attacked it. One little boy burst into tears and ran into his bikini-clad Mum's arms. Jiao became a little anxious herself, hoping there were no hungry fish near her. She did see something that looked like a fat sausage, lying on the sandy seabed she made sure she sidestepped that!

Thirsty and salty, she returned to their spacious and cheerful room. "Are you ready for some tea Mum?" she called as she came in the door, she beelined for the shower, turning it on to warm it up. Back in the room, the balcony was empty but there was Wenling, wheezing quietly, propped on her plump pillows, book and hands resting on her chest, her lips curved in a smile, sleeping soundly.

In the afternoon, Wenling wanted to swim in the pool. Children splashed and came whizzing down the slide, one after another. The Mum in Jiao worried that they would have an accident because they weren't leaving enough time between landings, but Wenling seemed happy just observing their joyful faces, listening to their whoops of excitement and chuckling at their mischievous antics. Jiao realised she wasn't the only one who missed the children being young. Seeing the world through their eyes, a world of wonder; one moment soaring on wings of delight, the next plummeting to the depths of sorrow. How lacklustre life had become without those little faces running through the door.

After the pool, a young 'red shirt' invited Wenling and Jiao to find out the secret recipe for 'Ike Mata'. It was a fish salad apparently and an island speciality. Wenling was enthusiastic so Jiao joined her, still dripping and wrapped in her generous hotel towel. Wenling surprised her again, producing a silky grey blue rectangle of material from her new beach bag and proceeding to wrap it around herself into a strapless dress, with the technique of a pro! Jiao noticed it had a white print ...seagulls! Perfect attire for a lesson on preparing raw fish!

The raw fish salad of which they each got a small bowl to taste, was surprisingly delicious ...chunks of lemony tuna and fresh island vegetables combined with pineapple, mayonnaise and coconut cream. Jiao carefully folded their copy of the recipe, to attempt herself on their return home. Appetites whetted they returned to their room to freshen up before dinner.

That night was 'Island Night', as the sign by the pool had informed them, with music, dancing and an Island feast. Jiao had bought them tickets.. With time to kill before the 7 pm dinner, she rang room service and ordered two tropical cocktails.

Although Chaoxiang was in the beer trade, Jiao and Wenling rarely drank any alcoholic beverage except the occasional glass of Juimiang, fermented sweet rice wine, scented with Osmanthus flowers. However, while they had watched the 'cooking class', Jiao had noticed the tall glasses filled with rainbow liquids and decorated with fruit and flowers being delivered on trays to other guests and she thought they would be a perfect accompaniment to watching their first sunset from their new beachside 'home'.

When the rap at the door came and a muffled island voice said "Madam" Jiao's heart skipped a beat. She slowly opened the door, searching the face of the young man holding their tray of exotic potions. He wore a green shirt with a golden flower print, obviously the colour for room service but while his eyes were friendly and strangely as green as his shirt, he was not the man she'd met on the beach who somehow had left her caught under his spell.

CHAPTER 9 FORBIDDEN FRUIT

The Island Banquet was a sumptuous affair. Long, draped tables had appeared in the centre of the lagoon side restaurant and were a blaze of colour, laden with mysterious dishes to choose from. Jiao wore a floaty yellow dress Chao had bought for her in Dubai, it reminded her of sunshine and being young. Wenling was looking regal in a new red and gold dress adorned with a shell necklace. They followed the shuffling queue of guests spooning a little of each delicacy onto their plates, until there wasn't any space left to squeeze on another morsel.

They had a table close to the stage where a Ukulele group were singing island songs; their fingers moved skilfully, quickly strumming and creating a joyful noise as Papa Jake had at the airport. Jiao wondered if they too would play "Welcome to my world'. She missed Weng Li Chan and wished she had found the courage to make this excursion a few years earlier and he and Lifen Chan could have sat at this table with them. They would have loved this place.

As it was Jiao and Wenling were alone at a table for two; a handsome young Australian couple were at the table close beside them. Jiao guessed, from the contented looks on their faces that they were newly-weds. She couldn't help tuning in to their conversation and gathered that the beautiful, bronzed girl with her curly dark locks, was of Rarotongan descent. Her accent was Australian, but she knew the names of the traditional dishes exclaiming "Rukau!" my Mum used to cook this, it's made from Taro leaves, hard to find back home. If you don't cook it right it scratches your throat like eating thistles!" Her tanned young blond man's eyes widened, and he looked at the dark green sinewy mush on his fork with a worried frown. The girl threw her head back letting out a carefree laugh, then ate a large mouthful, grinning as she chewed.

Jiao timidly tasted the mushy dark rukau. It was surprisingly delicious, a unique nutty flavour with a hint of chilli and coconut. "Poke!" their neighbouring diner exclaimed again, it's like jelly, mmm I think this is pawpaw flavoured and the sauce is coconut cream." Jiao searched her plate for the orange globs smothered in white cream and sprinkled with grated coconut. It was delicious! Definitely, something she would be return to the buffet for.

Jiao loved buffets; she always found choosing from a menu problematic, her sense of adventure would rise up inside her and she would want to try every dish that was new to her. Whatever she eventually decided upon, she would never enjoy to the full due to a gnawing dread that she had missed out on something more delicious. So, the Island Feast was her perfect type of meal. She continued to work her way through all the novel taste sensations on her plate. She tasted curried eel, Ike Mate, the raw tuna salad they'd had the lesson in making and 'Umukai', meat and vegetables which had been cooked, wrapped in banana leaves, in an 'Umu': an underground oven of wood and stone, more information she had gleaned from her neighbouring diner.

Some things she expected to be savoury were sweet; others she thought would be sweet were bitter or bland. The sea air had obviously given Wenling an appetite, normally a small eater, she had eaten her way through everything on her plate without a murmur.

She looked up at Jiao smiling happily, she had obviously enjoyed the new flavours and was feeling pleased with herself for polishing off the plate. Just then, the drumming began.

The mellow Ukulele band had left the stage and was now replaced by men in island shirts playing indigenous drums of different shapes and sizes. Jiao sat back to enjoy the spectacle.

A wild-looking man appeared wearing nothing but a piece of island cloth hanging between his legs, a flower garland and mini grass 'skirts' around his lower legs. He leapt on to the stage and began to shout in his native tongue. One of the drummers behind him, paused his drumming to shout out a translation. "Welcome everyone to a night of magic, a night of music and dance".

Exotic Cook island girls scantily clad in grass skirts, with plumes of bright feathers, fixed to their heads ran onto the stage, shaking their grass skirts while keeping their upper bodies straight and making graceful movements with their arms. The faster the drums beat, the faster their hips shook. They were beautiful young women, with long flowing hair and big round eyes, nothing but coconut shells covered their breasts and they had slim waists and strong wide hips. The rhythm was repetitive but somehow exciting and carnal. Just as this thought crossed her mind, the girls left the stage and four men came forward, it was the wild man and three more identically clad in cloth, grass with nothing but paua shell and flax necklaces covering their rippling chests. They were waving their hands and their knees almost knocked together as they moved them so quickly.

One of them looked strangely familiar ...it was him ...the buggy boy, the handsome young man on the beach. He looked at Jiao and winked. Jiao could feel her face begin to burn, if only it wouldn't do that. Wenling looked at her with raised eyebrows, so she avoided her gaze and kept her eyes firmly fixed on the stage.

She tried not to check out his body but under the stage lights, perspiration sparkled like morning dew, on his broad, island chest. Jiao lowered her eyes... his strong thighs and calves were taut with muscles as they moved faster and faster to the rhythmic drums. Jiao allowed herself to glance up at his face for a moment, his gaze was still fixed on her and her heart began to pound as fast as the drums.

The ladies returned to dance with the men. The provocative closeness of their bodies made Jiao wonder in the origins of this dance was some kind of ancient mating ritual. She felt a ridiculous sense of jealousy that it wasn't her beside 'her young man', she didn't even know his name. Was it her imagination or could she really feel his smouldering eyes searching for hers, even as he danced this sensuous dance with his exotic young partner?

The evening wound down with a children's dance troupe, each elaborate costume was in a different colour, a gaudy array of artificial grass skirts, island print tops, crown-like headdresses adorned with dyed feathers and painted shells. One of the girls reminded Jiao of Lihwa when she was younger. She imagined their mother's and grandmother's hours of labour to construct the elaborate outfits. She wondered if they competed with each other for the most striking design.

All the while Jiao tried to avoid scanning the restaurant for a glimpse of her secret heartthrob. After the performance, he had disappeared. The ukulele band resumed, and guests began drifting up and down to the dessert buffet, which had magically appeared during the show.

When they eventually completed the slow ocean-side walk back to their room, Wenling and Jiao both collapsed, exhausted onto their beds. But while Wenling once again fell into a peaceful sleep, Jiao tossed and turned restlessly. She dreamt of furtive dalliances under cover of darkness, of stolen kisses, of dancing on the sand and making love in the sea. She saw the face of a boy, whose heart felt so much older, searching her eyes, consuming her with his love. His face changed, it was Chaoxiang, he turned from her in disgust. She sobbed deeply in the darkness, she was alone and naked in the cold, cast away from her home, disowned by her family.

She awoke, a gush of wind had flung open the balcony door and cool gusts had ransacked their room; her covers had fallen to the floor leaving her exposed, a pitiful shivering ball on top of her icy crumpled sheet.

CHAPTER 10 FOOTPRINTS IN THE SAND

The morning eventually dawned and after refreshing herself with a hot shower, Jiao put on her bikini and a colourful translucent beach dress and headed to the beach to clear her thoughts.

A storm had indeed swept through during the night and yesterday's pristine beach was littered with palm fronds and coconuts. The ocean was bellowing in the distance, as it continued to batter the reef. Even the relatively docile waves within the lagoon seemed to be lapping with increased vigour. Watery sunshine pierced through the lingering cloud cover, casting an eerie glow.

Jiao stretched and then she began to walk briskly away from the hotel, her head full of questions. *Why had she brought them here? What was she looking for?* Of course, she'd wanted to bring Wenling for the health benefits of a warmer climate, she laughed to herself, *there was still a cool breeze this morning, maybe she'd chosen the wrong island!* She thought of the island man dancing, *maybe she hadn't! Was she so desperate that the first handsome man to look her way, had sent her into turmoil? It was like a war had started inside her, what she knew was right versus what she needed, what her heart longed for.*

On the choppy sand, Jiao noticed one set of footprints. They reminded her of the picture and poem that had always been on the bathroom wall in Mr and Mrs Chans Takapuna apartment. She knew it by heart...

Footprints in the Sand

One night I dreamed I was walking on the
beach with God. Many scenes from
my life flashed before me. In each
scene I noticed footprints in the sand,
sometimes two sets, other times only
one.

This bothered me because during the
lowest and saddest times in my life,
there was only one set of footprints.
So I asked God,

"God, you told me when I decided to follow you, that you would walk with me all the way. But I noticed during the most trying times there has only been one set of footprints. Why when I needed you most, were you not there for me?"

God whispered, "My child, I would never ever leave you! During your times of trial and suffering when you saw only one set of footprints it was then that I carried you."

Copyright Timothy Keith

The hotel complex was far behind her now and the beach had narrowed. Stepping over the leafy debris that was strewn across the thin curving strip of sand, Jiao rounded the corner and heard a surprised gasp. She had thought she was too late to see her Island man taking his morning run but there he stood dripping with water, having just waded out of the sea. His muscles rippled as he stooped to pick up a threadbare red towel, which he threw over his shoulder.

Then he stared at her, "It's you!" he said, looking pleasantly surprised. Jiao's heart was pounding in her ears and her skin tingled under his gaze.

She had to say something, so she said: "Isn't it cold to swim?" As soon as the words left her mouth, she felt foolish... they were on a tropical island, surrounded by a reef, of course, it wasn't cold.

"Warmer in than out," he said, then leaning forward gave his thick dark hair a wild shake, sending salty droplets everywhere, including onto Jiao's face. She blinked with surprise.

On seeing her face and realising what he'd done, the man broke into laughter. It was infectious and Jiao found herself laughing too, maybe her pent-up tension was releasing, because she couldn't stop, neither could he, they found themselves sitting beside each other on the sand still laughing.

Once they had caught their breath, their conversation began to flow. He said he thought he'd seen her before, but she assured him it was her first time on the island. Jiao also felt a strange sense of familiarity she couldn't explain. His name was Jimmy, Jimmy Parima, he had been on Rarotonga for four years, he was from Mangaia, another Cook Island. She complimented him on his dancing the night before, he explained that he was just helping out some friends, they'd been missing a male dancer and he'd stepped in.

He explained that the dancers were also from Mangaia and when he had first arrived on Rarotonga, the dance group had let him join them until he'd found himself full-time work. Now he worked at the hotel, he was live-in and often worked late shifts, but he enjoyed having his mornings off when he could enjoy being a tourist!

Jiao told him about her Mum and how the warmth helped her arthritis. About losing her Dad and how Wenling had supported her by sewing and embroidering. Jimmy had also lost his father when he was just 12, his father died at sea and he was the oldest child, so had become the head of the household; no wonder he seemed older than his years.

His mother ran a bakery which was difficult because the ship carrying flour only came every two or three months and sometimes if the sea was too rough, it would have to turn back.

She asked about his island and his face lit up as he described his family and the simple life he sometimes missed. One of his sisters also lived on Rarotonga, she was a receptionist at a nearby villa and was married to a customs officer. "We try and go back home every Christmas," he told Jiao, "it's always a joyous time."

Suddenly their conversation stopped, the morning sun was starting to break through the cloud and Jiao could feel the warmth on her skin. She could also feel the warmth of Jimmy's eyes as they travelled from her face, over her suddenly heaving chest, down her slim arms to her flat but throbbing stomach over her lightly bronzed legs, then back to rest on her hand. She felt like he had undressed her with his eyes and flushed with embarrassed excitement.

Jimmy's look, however, had changed, he was staring at the Cartier wedding band that Chaoxiang had bought for her shortly after they had arrived in New Zealand.

Wearing wedding bands had not been part of marriage in Shandong but Chao wanted them to embrace New Zealand life and culture, so true to his nature he'd bought her an extravagant ring, which he insisted she should wear on her left hand.

The ring was 18K yellow gold, set with 29 round, brilliant-cut diamonds and Jimmy was staring at it with a look of horror. "Are you engaged?" he asked.

For a moment she wanted to lie, to pretend it was just her and her Mum and this Island full of promises but she knew she couldn't. They were sitting so close, their skin was almost touching, one lean and their lips could have met but now she had to break the spell.

"It's worse than that, I'm married."

His eyes fell to the sand and she felt both their hearts sink as if she too had only just learnt of her situation. They sat in sad silence for a moment, then he gathered himself back together, his smile returned, and he spoke,

"Well I can't pretend I'm not disappointed, but the Lord knows best. I hope we can still be friends. I will try to keep my thoughts clean." He kept his eyes focused on her face and there was no mockery, he meant it.

She sighed a mixture of relief and disappointment. She'd so longed to be held in his arms; but at least he hadn't rejected her completely.

He leapt up. "I'll walk back with you." As they walked, the comfortable familiarity between them returned. Jimmy wanted to know all about Chaoxiang, how they had met, their family, their immigration to New Zealand. She described her house and Fred the gardener, she even told him some of the stories he had told her. Jimmy smiled at her, a guileless, open smile which shone from the depths of his sparkling brown eyes.

In a funny way, Jimmy reminded her of Fred. The warmth that radiated from him, the safeness she felt in his presence, the light in his eyes, the all-knowing assurance. As they neared Jiao's apartment, Jimmy bowed and waved his hand jestfully, "Well my Fair Lady, I will take my leave. Shall we meet again tomorrow?" Jiao laughed and agreed, "Same time, same place!".

Wenling had been observing them from the balcony. "Who was that young man you were with?" she asked, concern in her voice.

"Oh, that was Jimmy." Jiao realised the fear and yearning she had felt when she had left that morning, had dissipated, replaced by a pure kind of joy, the soaring joy of knowing and being known.

CHAPTER 11 COOKIE MAGIC

Jiao and Wenling were ready to venture out from their comfortable surroundings and decided to explore Avarua, the main town of the Island.

Fuelled by their tropical breakfasts, they stood under a palm tree outside the foyer entrance, waiting for the bus. Jiao had discovered that public transport was quite straight forward on this little island, there were two options: clockwise or anticlockwise and they ran hourly. As the town was only about ten minutes away in a clockwise direction, that was the one they needed and it was almost due.

After a few minutes, inhaling the floral scents that filled the air, the bus arrived. They settled themselves on plastic covered seats that had seen better days. The rattling, bumping and wind whistling through the jammed-open windows, made it impossible to converse, but they both had smiles on their faces as they listened to the driver singing over the din. He was singing old fashioned love songs, full pelt, as Jiao might do when vacuuming but she couldn't imagine doing that in front of a bus full of people. He seemed to throw himself into the dual role of driver and entertainer, serenading people as they entered and left the bus, much to the delight of most of the passengers. By the time they arrived at the 'main bus stop' outside a fudge and souvenir shop they were both feeling well shaken and happily stirred!

Wenling enjoyed pottering around the souvenir shop buying trinkets for Junjie and Lihwa. Jiao thought Junjie was a bit old to appreciate such things anymore but didn't say anything as her mum was obviously taking great pleasure in choosing them.

Wenling then discovered the homemade fudge and spent an inordinate amount of time choosing flavours, her wobbly joints forgotten in the face of sweet treats.

Eventually, bag full, she was ready to sit down in the adjacent café. They sat and sipped iced coffee watching the unusual flow of island traffic. Mainly scooters, laden with brightly clothed island men and women, some with a whole wad of children, squeezed between Mum and Dad, some with crates of live chickens or laden with shopping. Jiao loved the floral prints they wore, mirroring the lush flora of the island and the way both men and women adorned themselves with fresh flowers, woven in a wreath and worn like a crown or a single bloom stuck behind one ear.

She showed Wenling the frangipani body lotion she'd bought in the fudge shop, squirting some on her skin. She knew the scent would always conjure up memories of this enchanting island and the young island man who'd found a place in her heart.

Wenling was showing her the box of fudge she had bought for herself. "Try some watermelon flavour", the fudge was pink and green with black seed-like bits in; Wenling took a big chunk and was chewing it blissfully. She had such a sweet tooth, which probably explained why she had so few of her own teeth left. She still managed to chew through the fudge though!

She also showed Jiao the painted glass geckos she had chosen, one green with coloured spots for Junjie, the other pink and orange for Lihwa. Jiao had never seen the room Junjie shared at the campus. Chaoxiang had driven him on his first day, as Jiao had been taking Lihwa to a netball tournament the same weekend. Then Chao had visited him another time but hadn't told her until after the event. She wondered if his room was neat or messy. Did he have a shelf for ornaments? Probably not.

Lihwa's room was always tidy and she hated dust. She had a painted box in her cupboard where she kept her 'treasures'. This new trinket would probably be placed in this box and 'filed' on the shelf.

After their rest, Wenling was ready to investigate more shops. There was a small supermarket, with a busy flow of scooters pulling in and out of the parking bay outside. They could see it was popular with tourists and locals, most of the locals were departing with large boxes of frozen chicken, which they strapped precariously onto their mopeds. Wenling spotted the fresh fruit ice cream counter just inside the front doors, Jiao felt like she was the parent, telling her Mum to wait until they had finished shopping.

Wenling was glad she waited as they discovered a whole strip of the souvenir shops which she loved. They window shopped on island treasures before turning down a covered walkway, decorated with vases of feathers, strange tiki-like statues and an array of colourful windchimes. When the walkway opened, they felt like they'd entered the belly of a galleon, laden with bounty. There, Wenling bought herself a fan shell necklace. The lady serving explained to her Mum that it was a 'Parau' shell a genuine Cook Island mother of pearl shell, handwoven with 'Rito' – Young Coconut leaves, which fanned out around the shell, like dried grass.

It reminded Jiao of the necklaces the male dancers had been wearing and the 'grass skirts' round their calves. The image of Jimmy dancing half naked on the stage, came back to her, his eyes fixed playfully on hers. Suddenly she found her body heat rising, heart pounding and she had to remind herself that they were friends and would never be lovers.

She wondered if Chaoxiang experienced these feelings when he first met his beautiful young secretaries. Momentarily, for the first time, she felt sympathy for his weakness for young mistresses.

Clueless about her thoughts, Wenling was trying on an array of sunhats and wanting Jiao's opinion. She settled on a wide brimmed light straw hat with straw strands that fanned out like her necklace. The sun was high in the sky, so she put it straight on.

They walked back towards the bus stop, giving Wenling her chance to buy her long- awaited mango fruit ice cream from the supermarket. As she sat at the bus stop eating it, Jiao went into the stationers.

This was Jiao's sort of treasure trove, full of books, cards, pens and paper. She picked out some postcards to send to Lifen Chan, Fred and the children. Moving further into the shop, her eyes were drawn to the tabletop covered in books of all shapes and sizes. There were books on Cook Island flowers, local history, recipe books, schoolbooks, books full of stunning photography and interestingly, a book on Mangaia ... 'Mangaia and the Mission' by Peter H. Buck (Te Rangi Hiroa). Jiao was tempted to buy that one, but she needed to stop thinking about Jimmy, so instead she chose a large hardcover book of photography, 'Cookie Magic'. The shots had been taken throughout the Cook Islands, and leafing through a few pages, Jiao knew this book would give her great pleasure. She squeezed her way between loaded tables and shelves to the counter, where she noticed a small cardboard box full of bookmarks. She wanted a bookmark for her new book, so looking through she pulled one out, turquoise water lapping at a sandy shore and a poem in pretty font, she read the words ...

'Footprints

One night I dreamed I was walking along the beach with my Lord...'

That poem again! The one she had been thinking of just that morning. She stuck it on top of the book and the cards and paid with Cook Island dollars. The thick notes she had bought from her travel agent, were beautiful, printed in shades of green and orange with pictures of flowers and birds. It felt like toy money, as did the coins she received as change from the distracted shopkeeper; they were a lightweight, dull silver metal, some were wavy edged and some triangular much to her surprise.

By the time she emerged from the crowded labyrinth of the shop into the sunny street, her Mum, sitting at the bus stop, was crunching the last of her ice cream cone. A small crowd had joined her, awaiting the arrival of the clockwise bus.

They had decided during their time in the coffee shop to carry on clockwise and do a tour of the island back to the hotel. Jiao was hoping Wenling was fit for the bumpy ride, the complete circuit was only thirty-two kilometres, but it would still take a while as Jiao had noticed the speed limit was thirty kilometres per hour.

She needn't have worried as in the midst of the bellowing bus driver, the rattling bus and the warm ocean breezes, Wenling promptly fell into a bumpy sleep. Jiao put her arm around her mother, cushioning her frail body as much as she could. Gazing out the open window, she let her eyes drink in the beauty of the Island.

The town was relaxed but alive, with locals laughing, trading and going about their daily business, while tourists wandered around in pairs and groups, like her, taking in the sights. As the bus left the town, the trees thickened and they began passing a strange mixture of tumbled down old ruins, well maintained family homes with colourful tables and chairs on the veranda, some with large concrete graves in their gardens, pristine holiday bungalows. They passed an ancient-looking church with a spire, a resort entrance, a school, a makeshift home of dried woven palm leaves with a pig tied up outside. It was all so different to New Zealand and her home city of Qingdao.

Jiao's heart leapt at the sight of the bright flowers on the trees, yellows, oranges and reds, set against the backdrop of the majestic green mountain interior. They passed turquoise lagoons and the water sparkled in the sunlight, lapping the sandy white shore.

They continued on past fruit-laden stalls that also sold 'Cook Island donuts'. Jiao wanted to stop the bus and try one. She saw a sign pointing inwards to the thick bush lined track,

'Noni Juice 1.5KM'. She wished she could follow the dusty road and find out what Noni Juice was.

Gardens hidden behind foliage and a wooden sign 'Maire Nui Tropical Gardens' slipped by and another that said, 'WORLDS BEST CHEESECAKE'. She saw colourful Maraes, where children played on the swings and a large, imposing church painted white.

By the time they turned onto the climbing palm fringed road to their resort and she had woken Wenling, Jiao was feeling heady with all the new sights and smells.

CHAPTER 12 AN INVITATION

As promised Jimmy was waiting on the shore for her the next morning. He'd been for a swim and lay on the sand with his eyes closed. Jiao padded quietly down the beach and sat beside him. The sun was rising behind them and beads of water sparkled in his dark curly hair and ran down his perfect brown thighs. "I've been thinking..." Jiao jumped, startled at his voice, as he started speaking, his eyes still closed. "I would like to take you somewhere tomorrow morning."

"Where?" Jiao asked, wondering how he had known she was there, when she'd sat down so quietly. "Well, that's a surprise... for me to know and you to find out. I will pick you up at 9am."

"How did you know it was me?" Jimmy opened his eyes and looked at her with dreamy eyes. You smell like nothing I have ever smelt before. I wish you didn't. He turned his gaze from her and fixed them on the horizon.

She realised it was her perfume; it had always been her favourite scent, lotus flower. It was part of her morning ritual to dab a little of the expensive oil on her wrists and behind her ears.

Suddenly Jimmy jumped up, brushing the glittering sand from his shorts, "Come on, let's walk. No! Let's run!" He began to run down the beach and Jiao ran after him, hoping they weren't being watched. Their suite and many others had balconies facing over this part of beach. She didn't look back, so she didn't notice Wenling's disapproving face watching her, as she tried to sprint through the sand.

They kept running until they had left the hotel complex behind them, they ran past the spot where Jimmy had swum the day before, Jiao's legs felt strong and she realised the hours she had spent watching TV or reading a book on her cross-trainer had paid off. In the back of her mind she had wanted to be more attractive to Chaoxiang, so he would look at her again instead of younger women, but now here she was pleased to have strength and muscle tone beside a younger man who appreciated her looks and fitness!

Jimmy eventually slowed down as the beach became rocky and overgrown. He looked back at her. Her emerald beach wrap or 'pareu' as she'd been told they called it on the Cook

Islands, had slipped off as she'd run. Jimmy's eyes ran over her black bikini, down to her sandy ankles, she saw colour rising in his face and he turned away, heading for a rocky mound.

Feeling naked, Jiao tied the pareu over her bikini top, so instead of a skirt it became a strapless dress. Jimmy patted the flat piece of rock beside him and she joined him. They watched the waves break on the reef and Jimmy threw small pieces of rock into the flat sea causing loud plops. He gave Jiao a handful to throw. Jimmy talked about his childhood and how one day he would like children of his own. He was torn between returning to Mangaia and staying on Rarotonga.

In Mangaia his Mum was keen for him to take over the bakery, there his family would be known and sheltered, and his children could run around freely as he had done.

If he stayed in Rarotonga there were bigger schools, a college, even a polytechnic. "...or I could do what you did, leave it all behind and travel to unknown places... like New Zealand."

"You could stay with me!" Jiao blurted out before she thought about what she was saying.

Jimmy laughed. "Maybe one day, when I have a family of my own too!"

They wandered back slowly along the beach, collecting shells and chattering like carefree children. Jiao felt younger and more alive than she had for years. She wished she could bottle this time and take it back with her, to revive her in her dark and lonely hours.

She felt sad as he left her, but also excited, wondering what he had planned for the next morning.

When Jiao arrived back at their room, Wenling was sitting on her bed, dressed and ready for breakfast, with a definite scowl on her face. "Jiao you are a good girl and I don't often scold you but no good is going to come of meeting with this boy. You are acting like a besotted schoolgirl, he's not much older than a schoolboy either. It's very bad. Very bad!" She shook her head with a look of impending gloom.

"It's innocent Mum, he knows I am married, and we are just friends." Jiao said with more conviction than she actually felt. "I know I have you, but sometimes I need someone else to talk to. He's from Mangaia." Over breakfast she told Wenling more about Jimmy, his life on Mangaia, his hopes and dreams, but Wenling although interested, remained in a state of quiet concern.

It was a warm day, so they decided to visit the resort gift shop (Wenling could never resist a souvenir shop). Jiao bought herself an island print dress, in white with coral pink frangipanis and Wenling found a peacock design silk scarf and some petrol blue pearl earrings which she bought as a gift for Lifen. After that, they headed to the pool for a refreshing swim and some lunch, where they agreed they would participate in the afternoon activity of 'ei making'.

What they called 'leis' in Hawaii, were called 'eis' here. The 'l' apparently hadn't survived the ocean crossing ...Jimmy had laughingly told Jiao this, as well as that the canoe or 'Waka' as it is known in New Zealand Maori, in the Cook Islands is known as a 'Vaka'.

Jiao was telling her Mum these things as they were led by a red t-shirt activity man wearing a colourful crown of flowers, to a large table under a palm leaf shelter, which was piled with native greenery. Out of the corner of her eye Jiao saw Jimmy in his uniform, driving a buggy laden with baggage, seeing them he waved and smiled, Jiao waved back but Wenling looked away, her face stony cold.

CHAPTER 13 THE UNEXPECTED DESTINATION

The next morning, Jiao awoke early but lay in bed quietly hoping not to wake her mother and wondering where she could tell her she was going.

As she lay staring at the whitewashed ceiling, she found herself thinking of her father. Her earliest memory was of sitting on his knee in their modest rooms. He had a favourite chair, made of wood, 'Qing dynasty', he would say with pride, Wenling would roll her eyes, which made Jiao wonder if it really was, but her Father loved it and when he was sat in it, she loved it too!

He was always pleased when she jumped on his knee. She would sit there, her arms wrapped around his neck and he would smile and rock her gently or tell her a story in his soft, low voice.

On this particular day, the room was full of noise and bustle, Jiao's aunt, Jimo was there with her uncle, and her little cousins were running around their ankles fighting.

In the midst of the din and confusion, Jiao sat in her Father's arms, completely content and at peace, listening to his voice, which could transport her, like a magical book, to other worlds and dimensions.

Lying now, in her sterile hotel bed, in the cool of the morning, so many miles and years removed from him, her heart ached deeply.

Then she remembered her early days with Chaoxiang, how he had held her, burying his face in her hair, holding her tightly wanting to leave. She remembered the deep scent of him, how she would breathe him in; standing in the laundry in their first apartment in Qingdao, holding his shirt to her face, inhaling the smell of him, missing him even though he'd only just walked out the door.

Her heart shuddered, how alone she was now. No father to hold her, no husband who loved her, she was alone, adrift, clinging to futile fantasies, pinning her hopes on a boy whose heart she could only break. How could she ever abandon her children or Wenling?

She thought of locking the door to protect him from her, but her curiosity won out. Her father had always loved her curious, questioning mind but maybe now it would land her in trouble. Where was Jimmy going to take her? What would happen if they were really alone?

She slipped quietly from under her sheets and tiptoed to the bathroom; she closed the door and filled up the bathtub.

As she slipped under the warm bubbly water, her mind returned to the day they had knocked on their door, announcing to Wenling that her father was never coming home. She didn't hear the words, the men she had recognised as her father's work 'comrades', spoke in muffled voices, eyes downcast. Her mother wailed and they scuttled away, like cockroaches.

Her Mum had grieved loudly, the neighbours came in and out, joining in with the moaning, they looked pityingly at Jiao. Jiao couldn't cry but she remembered shivering in her bed, frozen and paralysed to her heart.

The warm peace that her father had always emitted was quickly displaced by the heavy despair of death and grieving. The lingering loneliness hadn't left her until she'd met

Chaoxiang. Even then, at times, her missing Father had felt like a hole in the atmosphere.

She wished Chao had met him and the children could have heard his stories and been loved by him too.

But Chaoxiang had revived her heart, had brought warmth and joy back into her life. She had felt adored again.

At least she had until that awful day. Coming in from the garden, tired and dirty after hours of clearing the ground, she had seen Chaoxiang's car and her heart leapt. His driver hovering in the hallway, had mumbled an awkward greeting as Jiao passed him. Hearing Chao upstairs, she ran up them and burst into their room. "You're home! How did the deal go?" Chaoxiang had been meeting with government officials and businessmen, trying to set up a two-way trade in gold with China. He'd even had to take on a full-time personal assistant.

Then she'd registered what he was doing. He had three large cases open on the bed and was removing all his items from their walk-in closet. Suits, shoes, shirts, ties, watches, jewellery, even his leisure wear.

Jiao's mouth had dropped open, "What are you doing?"

"It's best. I'm going to be doing a lot of entertaining. I'll visit when I can." He had avoided her eyes and when he did glance at her, when she stood and watched his chauffeur drive him away; his eyes were blank and cold.

For some time, the frozen feeling was almost more than Jiao could bear. It was like she had been thrown back into the past, once more paralysed by a grief that was beyond words. She avoided people. Even Wenling and Fred had been hard to face for a while. Sometimes at night, she would wake sobbing and shuddering but mostly she just held it in until it became normal again.

Jiao splashed her face with water, trying to wash away her thoughts. Why had all these memories filled her today? She needed to push them down and compose herself; she had to tell Wenling she was going out with Jimmy.

Wenling awoke as Jiao emerged from the bathroom in her favourite electric blue lingerie set. She quickly slipped on her smartest dress, then explained that she was going out for a bit. Wenling said little. She agreed to get room service and have breakfast on the balcony with her book, then she looked at her with her all-knowing eyes and said, "Don't let me down, daughter." Jiao hoped she wouldn't. She straightened the buttons of her collared dress, hoped her black sling-back shoes would be suitable for wherever they were going, then went outside to wait for Jimmy.

Jimmy appeared on time; he was wearing a shirt and long white trousers. Jiao felt pleased she'd dressed up. He admired her outfit and assured her that her shoes would be fine; it was just a short walk.

They walked down a narrow sand-swept road that ran between various bungalows belonging to the resort, coming out on a slightly wider, stonier one. They passed hire cars parked in a field and a man called a greeting to Jimmy, who gave him a salute.

Jiao stumbled a couple of times, so Jimmy stuck his elbow out in a very gentlemanly fashion, for her to hold on to. They were almost at the main circular road that encompassed the island, the one they had travelled on, when Jimmy slowed and said "This is it. This is my church. I wanted you to come."

The church was a simple structure with pressed metal sides, painted white and cream. It had an old, corrugated iron roof, rusting in places. Children ran in through a side door, but he took her around to the front, where a few other couples and families were arriving. There were two sets of eight windows, some boarded over, on either side of the open doors. There were no manicured lawns or church gates, just scrubby, sandy grass to the edge of the main tarmac road, probably why Jiao had passed it without noticing it was a church building.

Across the road was another patch of dusty grass which was quickly turning into a mini carpark as more churchgoers were arriving. Jimmy put his hand on her shoulder and steered her through some darting island children, dressed in their Sunday best, the girls in tailored dresses with matching ribbons in their hair and a boy in long blue trousers, with braces and a blue bow tie. In the window behind them, a blackboard perched, colourful chalk writing read: 'Sunday service. 9.30 am. All Welcome.'

"Hello Jimmy" shouted the oldest of the children as she stopped in front of Jimmy and gave Jiao a long curious look. Jiao's skin crept, she suddenly felt self-conscious and exposed. How had she ended up here; so far from home with a man half her age, wishing he was walking her into a cheap room not his church and feeling like this round-eyed girl could read her mind? What was a 'service' anyway?

Jiao lowered her eyes as they passed under the doorway. She didn't see the faces of the large brown hands that shook hers firmly but shuffled forward wishing she could melt into the ground.

Sensing her discomfort Jimmy quickly ushered her into a chair at the back of the neatly arranged rows near the back of the room. Her heart was pounding, and she didn't know why she felt so afraid.

Her memories of attending the Tsaoist temple with her father, though distant were good ones. This was different though. She was not the innocent child she had been then.

She had heard Fred and even Lifen talk about the principles of Christianity. They were both good people, but **she** couldn't be called 'good' anymore. She had failed as a wife, as a mother, even as a daughter, ready to bring disgrace and embarrassment on Wenling.

Jiao was disappointed that Jimmy had brought her to a church instead of his bed. She was a treacherous woman ready to do anything to ease the ache inside.

Staring down at a pink spot on the blue carpet she gritted her teeth and forced back her tears. Was this a trick? Had Shanti, the God of Judgement found out about her darkened heart and set this up to expose her?

CHAPTER 14 THE ENCOUNTER

Jiao's eyes were still firmly planted on the floor when the music began: a guitar and a keyboard, someone gently beating a drum. They weren't all keeping time and it sounded a little discordant to her ear but then a small quivering voice began to sing, quietly at first but building in confidence and volume. "I've heard a thousand stories..." Jiao's mind immediately took her back to her Fathers knee, if he had lived, he probably would have told her a thousand stories by now.

The next words she heard, caught her off-guard: "You're a good, good father" She looked up and a tubby island lady, who still appeared a little self-conscious, suddenly looked Jiao straight in the eye and repeated the line, "You're a good, good father and I'm loved by you."

Jiao looked over her shoulder but there was no one there, they were in the back row and it felt like the lady whose bashful eyes were suddenly brimming with love and tears, was singing it to her. Jiao stared back at her, confused and disarmed, how could she know about her Father or how he had loved her? Why was she singing these words in a church?

The lady sang on, over the congregation but her gentle gaze returning to Jiao, "I've seen many searching for answers far and wide but I know we're all searching for answers only you provide 'cause you know just what we need Before we say a word...."

Jiao looked back down at the pink speck on the blue carpet, her heart was pounding, her head spinning. What were they singing about? Who knows what we need before we say a word?

What kind of God were they singing to, who would care about her needs, she, who had been given so much and made a mess of it all? What kind of a God was this that they would call a good father?

She **knew** what it was to have a good Father, and she'd never heard of any God that could love like that. She found herself stifling a deep sob, much to her embarrassment. Jimmy put his arm out and patted her shoulder, which only added to her discomfort.

The song ended and after some general announcements the preacher got up to speak. He was short and stout, dressed in a boldly printed green shirt. Jiao was curious as to what he would say. The only church she had been in was the one in Takapuna where Mrs Chan had held her husband's funeral. It had been a formal, sombre service with a choir and a man in robes had spoken. This church was different.

The preacher cleared his throat, glanced around and then began:

"The story of the Loving Father."

Jiao felt a shiver go down her spine, was someone reading her thoughts?

"Abraham Lincoln said, 'The strength of a nation lies in the homes of her people."

Maybe that's why I feel so weak thought Jiao because my home is broken.

My story is of a man, reared in a wonderful
and beautiful home, the preacher

continued, A God-fearing home. The
Father loved his sons and they
worked with him on his land.

Jiao thought how she would have loved it if Junjie or Lihwa
had ever joined her working on their land but the only
person who had ever worked alongside her was Fred.

"One day one of the sons went to his
Father and said, 'By law when you die
you will give me one-third of your
estate, but I want it now.' He wanted
the pleasures of this world …he was
unsatisfied.

Many of us are unsatisfied with the way we
were made, the way we look, our
education, our lives, our partners, our
inner selves…"

Jiao thought of Chaoxiang and how he always wanted
something more, she thought of herself, her personality, her
lack of education, the emptiness she felt day and night.

"There's something lacking, and we don't know what it is.

Like the girl at college, she was crying and crying. They couldn't find out what was wrong, finally they brought her parents and eventually she blurted out, 'I want something, and I don't know what it is.'

Almost everyone is searching for something and doesn't know what it is. People think they'll find it in power, in money, in love or sex.

So, the son left his father, ignoring his advice to stay. He went to the city and enjoyed the high life. He partied and spent all the money until his money ran out. His so-called 'friends' turned from him. In desperation, he got a job feeding pigs. The bible say's 'He began to be in want'."

Jiao was surprised to hear that this story was actually in the Bible. Fred had never mentioned this one!

"It is impossible for us who were made in
eternity ever to find anything in this
world to satisfy our souls and yet the
Bible says, for those who know the
Lord, 'I shall not want'."

"He made you in His image. It doesn't
matter what you've done. He loves
you as His child."

"This man who had tried to fill his soul
with the world had ended up a slave
to sin. You are either a servant of
God or a slave of Satan."

"Your soul, your spirit, living there in your
body, for which you are responsible,
is more important than all the gold or
all the riches in the world."

Jiao was thinking of Chaoxiang now and wished he could hear what she was hearing; she longed for her husband to be beside her, instead of this fresh-faced, clear-eyed youth. She glanced at Jimmy sitting beside her, he was relaxed and comfortable, his eyes on the preacher, his head tilted to one side listening.

"What shall it profit a man to gain the
world but lose his soul?"

"You stand today at the crossroads. It's not
easy to serve God, the narrow road
leads to eternal life, but you have to
come by a narrow gate."

Fred had told her that he wasn't afraid to die, that he was looking forward to eternal life with Jesus. Jiao hadn't understood. How was he so sure of an eternal life? That he wouldn't get reincarnated into a dog or a garden slug? Anyway, how did you even enter the narrow gate?

"You have to come to the foot of the cross
and say to God, 'I have sinned. I'm
sorry for my sin. I believe Christ Jesus
is the Son of God and died in place of
me, that I can be reconciled to my
Heavenly Father."

Jiao's heart began to race! Had he heard her thought? Should she do it? There was a wooden cross, draped in what looked like a white lace tablecloth. Thankfully before she could decide how to respond, the speaker went on.

"This young man had had all these experiences; now he's sitting with the pigs, hungry to eat even the pigs' food.

He comes to his senses and realises he has sinned against Heaven. He is sorry and decides to go home and see if his Father will let him be one of his servants.

The Father sees his son, stumbling down the road, hungry and ragged and he runs down the road and throws his arms around him.

The Father ordered a robe for him, a ring for his finger.

Our Father in Heaven is saying to you
today, you are my son, you are my
daughter, I love you, come home."

The preacher continued to speak about the brother who had been with his Father the whole time, how his heart was hard and he thought he was earning the Father's love through service, but all Jiao could feel, was wave after wave of love washing over her.

She didn't know where it was coming from, but she closed her eyes and said, 'God, I don't know you but I do know I have made a mess of my life and if you are really there, I need you to help me.'

As she silently mumbled these words another great wave of indescribable love washed over her, and she fell to her knees and sobbed. She cried and cried and all the pain and disappointment of losing her Dad, of losing Chao's love, of her children slipping away from her just poured out and she couldn't stop it.

Her body shook, her heart physically ached, her head pounded, but then it happened. She felt Father's arms around her. Not her earthly Dad, but the same peace and comfort she had known with him. She could feel arms around her, gently rock her. She heard his voice, soft and kind, "I'm here Jiao, I'm your Father and I have always loved you."

The tears continued to flow down her cheeks. When she opened her eyes to look for Jimmy, the bashful lady who had been singing and another island 'mama' were patting her with their hands and crying with her. Instead of embarrassment Jiao experienced another tidal wave of love, rushing through her, filling her from her head to her toes.

After some time, Jiao wobbled to her feet. She felt momentarily self-conscious but the only looks her way were warm smiles. Children were running around with food in their hands, completely oblivious of Jiao and her supernatural encounter.

Jimmy, who had been beside her throughout, had now turned and was standing talking loud and cheerfully to a solid, bright-faced man with a beard.

The singer took Jiao's left hand in both hers and the other older lady put her arm around her, ushering her towards a spread of food. Jiao's head was a bit muggy from all the crying, but her body felt light and she was ravenously hungry. The Island Mama thrust a plate in her free hand and loaded her up with fresh doughnuts, pawpaw and egg sandwiches, then they led her to some seats along the side of the main meeting room.

"I'm Tanya," said the singer, "Jimmy's sister." Then she whispered in her ear. "It's true, He really loves you." Jiao looked back at her alarmed, what had Jimmy told her? "I'm talking about our Heavenly Father. You felt it didn't you? He really loves you and He wants you to know it."

Tears escaped Jiao's eyes again, this time they were tears of happiness. This was real, there was a God out there and what's more, he loved her like a Father.

She wolfed down the doughnuts which were more delicious than any she had ever eaten, not really sweet but fresh and doughy with a hint of coconut, then she ate the egg sandwiches and ended with the sweet pawpaw. Tanya laughed, "Being in His presence always makes me hungry too! Have you met the Lord before?" Jiao shook her head, still amazed at the morning's events.

Tanya proceeded to tell her about Jesus, God's son, who had died for our sins and to end our separation from God the Father. "When he rose from the cross before he ascended to be with His Father, he left his Holy Spirit to be with us, until He returns. When we accept Jesus as our Saviour, the Holy

Spirit is able to live in us. He is our comfort, our guide, our strength in times of trouble."

"When my father died, I wanted to die too. I was young but I missed him so much I just wanted the pain to stop. I even waded out as deep as I could in the lagoon and tried to drown myself, but Jimmy found me and carried me home."

Jiao remembered the deep despair that had engulfed her when she'd lost her Father.

"But then one day a boat arrived, and some white people got off. One of them was a lady with curly yellow hair and sparkling blue eyes, something about her attracted me and I followed her like a puppy dog." Tanya laughed a sweet musical laugh. "She had a guitar and she sat under a palm tree and began to sing, strumming her guitar. She sang about how my Father loves me and I felt his love wrap around me like a blanket. I will never forget that day." As she remembered Tanya's face seemed to soften and glow.

"I didn't want her to leave but she promised me my Heavenly Father would never leave me, that his Holy Spirit would stay with me and I would never be alone again.

She was right, I never felt alone again, and the darkness lifted. It's like I could breathe again. She taught me songs to sing and when she came back a few years later, she even brought me a ukulele with 'T' for Tanya painted on it.

I will always be thankful to her but most of all I'm thankful to my Father in Heaven, who sent his son to die, so I could live my life close to Him."

It was a lot for Jiao to take in, but she did truly feel as if a dark cloak of heaviness had been lifted from her and she hoped it would never return.

When she was ready to leave, Tanya squeezed her in a hug and said, 'We're sisters now you know. All God's children are brothers and sisters and He definitely loves you, sis!'

As she and Jimmy started walking up the gentle incline towards the hotel, he shared with her about his first encounter with the Lord.

"I still think you are the most beautiful woman I ever met," he told Jiao as they neared the steps to her room, "but maybe the Lord brought you into my life so you could find Him and we could be brother and sister here on earth and friends for eternity!"

"Maybe." said Jiao as she climbed the steps and turned to wave goodbye.

CHAPTER 15 FAMILY

Wenling's reaction was not what Jiao had expected. Instead of anger, her face showed relief. She didn't begin to admonish her but began to describe how Lifen Chan had told her about Jesus and Father in Heaven, when Weng Li had died.

At first Wenling had been afraid, after all, Jiao's father had been taken from them because of his Tsaoist beliefs, a century old Chinese religion, what danger could this western religion bring to them?

Lifen had told Wenling how her and Weng Li had both come from Christian families but in their hometown, they had kept this a secret and had attended an underground church. They had literally met in a large cave quite far away from their village. Other believers came many miles and sometimes the meetings would last all day and all night, but they had always left feeling filled to overflowing with life and love and hope.

Their daughter had also been a Believer and although the grief of losing their only child would never end, they knew that she was safe, and they would be reunited again.

Even losing her husband had been bittersweet for Lifen, for though she missed him deeply, she knew she would be with him again in better place and that he would be re-united with their beloved daughter.

Wenling opened the romance she had been reading and out dropped a small booklet. On the front was written in Mandarin, 'The gospel of Mark'. Jiao reached down to pick it up for her. "What is this?"

'Lifen gave it to me. It's from the Bible, the story of Jesus: what he said and did." It had a thin ribbon inside it and Wenling opened the page where the ribbon was.

"Listen to this!" She began to read. "Then His mother and His brothers came, and standing outside, they sent word to Him and called Him. A crowd was sitting around Him and told Him, 'Look, your mother, your brothers, and Your sisters are outside asking for You.' He replied to them, 'Who are My mother and My brothers?' And looking about at those who were sitting in a circle around Him, He said, 'Here are My mother and My brothers! Whoever does the will of God is My brother and sister and mother.'"

"What can it mean?" Wenling pondered. "Yes, Lifen is like a sister to me, but you will always be my daughter. How could another be your mother?"

They discussed this and many things about Jesus and Father God, Jiao felt like the air of their little living space was alive with excitement. She ordered her Mum a large fried rice with shrimp and some coconut pie which the room service boy delivered with a cheerful smile rewarded by Jiao's generous tip.

They sat out on the balcony in the shade of the gently swaying palms and talked about the wonders of nature and the world around them. Jiao found the book of Genesis audio book on her phone and they started listening to it while Jiao finished her Mum's rice and Wenling enjoyed her sweet coconut pie topped with cool ice cream.

They listened to the first three chapters, then Wenling was tired and ready for a siesta. Jiao closed the magenta curtains while Wenling sighed contentedly and sunk into her pillows.

Looking in the drawer of the desk, Jiao found the headed writing paper and hotel pen. The story of Adam and Eve was fresh in her mind. God had made Eve as a companion to Adam and said that man would leave his Mother and Father and 'cleave' to his wife.

Jiao looked up the word cleave and found the dictionary meanings: '1. to adhere closely; stick; cling (usually followed by to). 2. to remain faithful (usually followed by to).'

As she had listened to the deep male voice reciting the first chapters of the Bible, Jiao had felt a prompting in her spirit to write to Chaoxiang. She needed to tell him what had happened today, but also to be honest about how she felt about his unfaithfulness and his abandonment of her in every way except financial.

She sat back out on the comfy cushioned chair on the balcony and she thought back to their first home together in Qingdao. Softly biting her bottom lip, she began to write...

Dear Chao,

I am sitting here listening to the waves crashing on the distant reef and I remember the distant sound of the sea as we made love in our apartment in Qingdao. It feels like a lifetime away, a different me, a different you.

I thought you would always hurry home to me, that I would be your companion and comfort as you were mine.

I thought arriving to New Zealand, that being in a new land would bring us closer, but I was wrong. In Takapuna I was starting to make a life, learning to drive, enjoying the beach, getting to know the Chans, the children were happy, but then you uprooted me without ever asking my opinion.

Moving to Manakau I was so unhappy, so were the children. I think I would have died of loneliness without Wenling's company and support..

When you took your belongings from our room, my heart broke again like it had all those years ago when I lost my Dad. I thought I would never recover, and in some ways I haven't. I have just been existing not living.

What does all the grandeur of an expensive house, cars and business deals mean, if there is no love, if the family is broken, if the marriage is broken?

Coming here, I met a man who made me feel visible again. He wanted to spend time with me, to listen to me. He wanted to love me, but he is a good man and knowing I am married, he took me to meet his Father.

It is not what you imagine. He took me to his church, and I met a Father I didn't know existed. It sounds crazy but I felt his arms around me, I heard His voice. It is hard to believe that the Father of Creation, of Heaven and Earth, could care about me, but I believe it is true. We are all His children, he created us too, and if we will just turn from searching in all the wrong places, He will receive us back into His family.

I cannot explain how different I feel. Even if you and the children don't care about me anymore, I know I will never be alone. My Father loves me, and I have a family here and wherever I go, because we share the same Father. Even Fred and Lifen, I have realised are my family now.

I also want to say sorry to you, for being unfaithful in my heart. Nothing happened between myself and Jimmy, but I wanted it to.

In my heart of hearts, all I really want is to love and be loved by you, my husband.

God created man to be close to his wife, to be faithful to her. You may search for happiness in riches, in status, in false friends and beautiful women, but there is only way to find it. To come home to the one who made you and get your soul right with Him. It doesn't matter what you have done, He still loves you and wants to set you free.

Jiao didn't know what else to say, so she signed off,

'体健康' 'Good Health',

Yours,

Jiao

After carefully folding the letter, Jiao penned a few words on her postcards to Junjie, Lihwa, Fred and Lifen. She found herself apologising to Junjie and Lihwa for not being the Mum they needed. She felt a new outpouring of love for them both and tried to put it in words. To Fred and Lifen she was able to write that she had met their Heavenly Father in the most unexpected way; as she wrote, she couldn't wait to see them face to face, she suddenly had so many questions for them.

Once finished, she tiptoed past the quiet snores of her mother, out the door and down the slope to the world outside. She went to reception where they gave her an envelope and directed her to the shop for stamps, then she delivered the stamped addressed letters and cards back to the receptionist to post.

Later when Wenling awoke, they swam in the pool, showered and ordered dinner by the waterside, the whole time they talked about Jiao's experience that morning, the things Lifen had shared with Wenling and the things they had learned from the first chapters of Genesis.

Jiao enjoyed her Mother's company that night, more than ever before, it reminded her of the joy she had felt when her Father had told her his stories.

On their slow walk back to their room, Jiao felt like all her senses were heightened, she saw the details in the leaves of the lush tropical flora, the evening sun casting shadows on the rocks, wobbly hermit crabs scuttling on the sand, chased by squealing children, the salty smell of the mighty ocean. She felt awed and amazed at the scale of their world and the intricacy too.

Later, standing naked before the bathroom mirror, having enjoyed a soak in their corner bath, for the first time, Jiao saw the beauty of her own creation. She imagined Eve in the garden, before the serpent deceived her, her and Adam, walking with God, unashamed.

CHAPTER 16 'PITO'

The following days on the Island, passed too quickly. Jiao, with encouragement from Jimmy, hired a car from his friend with the car lot beside the church; a little turquoise Nissan Micra with a sunroof, Jiao really enjoyed the freedom it gave them.

Jimmy's sister, Tanya and her husband Hehu invited Jiao and Wenling to their home whenever Tanya wasn't working. She was expecting another baby so had cut her hours down to a few short shifts a week. It was only a few minutes' drive from the hotel on the interior side of the main island road. Down a turnoff, then a dusty driveway, there's was a simple home.

Tanya and Hehu's house was a wooden hut with concrete floors and a tin roof. Inside were just three rooms, two bedrooms and a living room with a round dining table where the children did their homework each afternoon.

The kitchen was an outdoor area covered by a corrugated plastic roof, there was a fridge-freezer, a washing machine and an enormous enamel sink, Tanya said it doubled as a baby bath, above it was a splattering old tap, dripping with rust. Her cooking area was a long rickety wooden bench covered in a plastic tablecloth. Under the bench were plastic boxes where she kept her food.

There was a hose with a shower head fixed to a tree near the kitchen. The first time Jiao and Wenling visited, Hehu arrived home from work, took off his uniform in the kitchen, put it straight into the top loader washing machine, then stepped outside in his underwear to shower in the garden. Jiao and Wenling both got a shock. Noticing their faces, he laughed, picked a bird of paradise flower that was growing beside him, and stuck it behind his ear. "Is that better?" he asked, Jiao and Wenling let out their embarrassment in peals of laughter.

The children, a boy and a girl, Mako aged 6 and Kimiora aged 5, loved to play in the tasselled linen hammock that hung between the palm trees, wild chickens ran free over the island and the children could regularly be heard whooping and screaming as they chased them out of the house. Once they found an egg in the bushes and proudly presented it to Tanya, she quietly told Jiao that they wouldn't be eating it as she didn't know how old it might be.

Another time they returned from their scavenging with three bedraggled kittens, Tanya wasn't happy, but Hehu said, "Let them play". So, the sleepy kittens stayed, and the children carted them around like floppy rag dolls.

Jiao and Wenling spent many happy hours sitting under the shade of the hand- woven palm fronds on the makeshift wooden deck Hehu had hand made from wooden pallets. Two old sofas and a lazy boy were draped with tropical island cotton throws, blue and green 'Ara or Fruit Salad' leaves as Tanya called them, 'Monstera Deliciosa' to Jiao, with white hibiscus flowers printed all over them. An enormous, solid bamboo and glass coffee table stood between the sofas, over which Tanya often threw a lacy white cloth and filled it with plates of fruit, a pile of doughnuts, or pineapple pie.

They drank fresh coconut juice out of green coconuts which Tanya produced from her fridge. Cool and refreshing, Tanya told them "nu" (as she called it) contained natural hydrolytes, gentle on the stomach it was good for babies and sick people too. Jiao and Wenling didn't need any convincing; it was the perfect drink on a tropical afternoon or evening.

One day they watched Tanya's son and daughter climb coconut trees by gripping their legs and arms around the trunks. They were competing to see who could get the most coconuts. Wenling spotted them first and pulled herself up out of the lazy boy to wave her stick telling them to get down. "Mind out Tapuna va'ine (Grandmother) they shouted, they had already reached the fronds and began throwing down young coconuts, Wenling quickly got herself back onto the safety of the deck.

Shortly after, Tanya came out the house praising the children and reassuring 'Tapuna Va'ine' that the children were good and careful climbers. "Their father taught them," she told them, "but his 'kopu' is getting too big for him to get up there now" she laughed, pointing to her belly.

When Hehu came home, he was very pleased with the children's bounty and quickly donned his 'pareu', a cotton wrap around his waist, and then began husking the coconuts on a sharp stake that was sticking out of the elephant grass, then fetching a machete, cleanly sliced off the tops. Jiao and Wenling suddenly realized the process that had been undertaken, for each of their chilled refreshments to 'magically' appear from Tanya's refrigerator!

One night, Hehu cooked fresh fish over an outdoor fire, his friends had caught them from the other side of the reef. Tanya made potato salad with mayonnaise, cooked frozen vegetables stirred through it and a boiled egg finely grated on the top. Jiao thought this was a strange island dish, but the children loved it, running back barefoot with their empty bowls for refills, like hungry, little wild things.

One particularly hot day, Tanya presented the children with a fold out plastic paddling pool, they quickly got to work, filling it up under the outdoor shower with buckets. After a few buckets had been emptied over each other's heads amidst screams and laughter, the children laid peacefully in the water, under the shade of the trees, spotting images in the clouds. Jiao, Wenling & Tanya all remembered doing the same thing as children. They decided it was probably a universally shared childhood pleasure.

Afterwards the children made mud pies, chocolate ice creams and cappuccinos for the adults, mixing their pool water with the rich dark dust scooped from between the lush greenery. They gave the adults coinage of silvery round shells they had found on the beach, to pay for their 'cafe' orders. Tanya reminded her offspring to count them carefully and give the right change.

One afternoon, Jiao and Wenling arrived unannounced. They had driven into town and picked up two large boxes of groceries from the supermarket, as a thank you for the family's hospitality. Strangely, the place seemed deserted but then they heard a whimper, a grief-stricken wail, followed by distressed mewing.

Rushing into the house, Jiao beheld a giant centipede, over a metre long, cut in two on the concrete floor, the large machete lying discarded beside it. "Tanya" she called looking into the children's room from where the noises came. Poor Kimiora was wailing inconsolably, Mako was hugging and patting her, staying brave and strong, determined to console his little sister. Tanya seemed upset, her face was drawn and her hands protectively covered her unborn child.

"What has happened?" asked Jiao. Kimiora held up the small limp body of the creamy, white kitten, "Tiare is dead." she sobbed, tears streaming down her cheeks, "Mummy killed the centipede, but it was too late."

Jiao helped the children dig a grave for Tiare, then they both sat with Wenling on the deck planning a ceremony. Kimiora wrote a song for the little animal and Mako prepared a speech.

Tanya and Jiao unpacked the groceries and began to prepare a meal. Jiao could tell that Tanya was still shaken. "What is it sister?" she asked. Tanya always called Jiao 'sister', we are sisters in Christ she would say and squeeze her hand. This was the first time Jiao had naturally called 'sister' back, her heart went out to her normally joyful companion.

"What if it had been the baby?" Tanya gasped, the fear filled her eyes, her hands shook. Unexpectedly, Jiao, not usually a touchy person, took Tanya's hands in hers and began to pray. She had never prayed aloud before, but the words poured out of her and a power surged through her. 'Father God, please take this fear away from my sister. Keep her unborn child safe. Protect her children this day and all the days to come. Bless this family and this home.'

Tears ran freely now down Tanya's face, she took Jiao in her arms, 'Thank you, the fear has lifted.

After Hehu and Jimmy arrived on their mopeds, a funeral took place for Tiare. Holding the two remaining kittens, a smoky grey and a black one, Mako spoke his farewell speech and Kimiora sang her song with quivering voice, then the remaining two kittens were ceremoniously fed a feast of rice and chicken before Mako sombrely led the adults back to their seats for their own meal of island style curry and rice.

Through all these island days and nights, Jiao and Wenling felt embraced into this family as if they had always been there. It was inexplainable. Conversation and laughter flowed freely, the children called Jiao 'Aunty' or 'Whaea Jiao' and Wenling 'Grandma' ... 'Tapuna Va'ine', or even sometimes 'Lao Lao', as they liked the sound of the Chinese name for Grandma. Everyone respectfully listened to anything Wenling had to say with great interest and attentiveness, they held her in high esteem, as an elder.

The Pastor of the church and his wife came to visit. He took his time to answer Wenling and Jiao's questions about the faith. He asked Jiao if she was sorry for sinning against her Father in Heaven and if she believed Jesus was the son of God who had died for her. She said she did. He asked her if she wanted to be baptised in the name of Jesus. Jiao did so they fixed a date and he told her to bring a towel.

When the day came, Jiao was nervous, but knew that she never wanted to lose the joy and peace that she had felt since her encounter with her Father. It was early afternoon and Jimmy and Hehu had both taken time off work to be there. Tanya and the children were happy and excited and Wenling was curious but also a little sad because she didn't feel ready to take such a step.

As soon as the pastor and his wife arrived in their rusty old jeep, they all traipsed along the dirt road to the beach. The Pastor walked Jiao into the water up to her knees, Hehu walked in too and stood at the other side of her, then the Pastor said, "I baptise you in the name of Jesus". Before she knew it, she had been immersed and raised from the water in the Pastor and Hehu's strong arms. As she stood there, dripping and cool, the little group, gathered on the waterside, raised their voices in joyful song. Jiao felt a darkness leave her, a darkness she hadn't known was inside her. As it did, she felt more alive than she'd ever felt.

After her baptism, they all returned to Tanya and Hehu's amidst much laughter and more singing followed by feasting. The pastor and his wife presented her with a book: 'the Holy Bible in English and Chinese'. "I have found that this book while always raising more questions, also answers the ones we have' he said. "As it is written, 'His ways are not our ways' and 'now we see dimly and only know in part, but one day we will know fully even as He fully knows us.' I don't have all the answers. I don't believe any of us will until His return, but I do know, ours is a good God, a God of love and light who fully knows and loves us despite that!" He laughed an easy laughter tinged with real joy. "Your next step is to be filled with the Holy Spirit." he told her.

Jiao would never forget the moment she had chosen to become a Believer in Christ, a Follower of the Way, in front of her newfound family. Neither would she forget, those nights, as the sun began to set, when Tanya fetched her guitar from her room. Sometimes the children would follow her cue, running to get their painted ukuleles. Hehu, comfortable in his cotton 'pareu', would perch on the edge of the sofa, his drum held between his knees. Then they would begin to play, singing hearty songs, sometimes in English, sometimes in their own language, sometimes just simple refrains repeated. Once they sang a song 'God's not dead, No! He is alive' They sang and shouted as loud as they could Mako banging his chest with his fist as he sang 'I feel it in my hands, then stomping his feet with all his might to ' I feel it in my feet' then Kimiore did a full body jiggle, waving her arms as she sang, ' I can feel it all over me.' Wenling tried to suppress her giggles at the sight of them. Hehu beat his drum, loud and clear for all the neighbourhood to hear. Jiao felt a stirring, as if to war, like a battle for their souls had been raging all along but she had only just woken from her sleep to realise.

Each night, they spoke to Father God, as if He were sitting around that table with them. They talked to Him about their day, asked advice on decisions, cried out for a friend to be healed, for a neighbour to be blessed, for justice in a court case. They opened their bibles and read a verse, then they would discuss what it meant, even the children would have their opinions.

Sometimes if he had a night off, Jimmy would turn up, Jiao was always pleased to see him, but realised she was incredibly happy whether he came or not.

The night before Jiao and Wenling were to fly back to New Zealand, nobody wanted the night to end. The sun had long sunk behind the trees, and mosquito coils and citronella candles were burning at each corner of the table. Mako was curled up beside Wenling, his head resting on her leg while she gently stroked his hair, Kimiore had fallen asleep in Jiao's arms listening to her Mothers gentle melodies and the rhythmic beating of her Fathers drum.

Wenling closed her eyes, but from her smile Jiao could tell she was drinking in the moment. Tanya began to sing, joined by Hehu's deeper tones...

> We are heirs of the Father.
>
> We are joint heirs with the Son.
>
> We are people of His Kingdom.
>
> We are family, we are one.

We are washed,

We are sanctified.

We are cleansed by His blood.

We are born of the Spirit.

We are children of the Lord.

We are members of His body.

We are objects of His love.

We're partakers of His holiness.

We are citizens of heaven above.

We're partakers of His suffering.

We're partakers of His grace.

We shall meet Him to be like Him.

We shall see Him face to face.

We are longing for His coming.

We are looking to the skies.

We are watching, we are waiting,

We shall dwell with Him, we shall rise.

We shall reign with Him forever.

Men and angels shout and sing.

For dominion has been given

To the family of the King.

Jiao listening, drank the words like sweet wine, she felt intoxicated with deep joy and a hope she couldn't even put into words, but at the same time, waves of sorrow washed over her at the thought of leaving these people and this place that had become a part of her heart.

As if hearing her thoughts, Tanya looked up at the end of the song, tears streaming down her cheeks, "It is true." she said, "We are family, we will always be joined by the blood of Jesus. However far apart, we will still be one. Even if we never meet again on this earth, our inheritance is the same and we have forever to look forward to, reining with the King!"

Jiao didn't fully understand her friend's words, but something in her spirit stirred.

Tanya got up and squeezed herself next to Jiao on the sofa, "We are your 'Pito' as we say in Mangaia, your 'tribe', your 'royal family.

CHAPTER 17 THE END?

Standing on the tarmac in the afternoon heat, Jiao looked up, with a sinking heart, at the shell of a beast that was to fly them back to Auckland Airport, with a sinking heart. The plane was much smaller and older than the one they had come in and she felt a terrible sense of foreboding.

The whole check-in process had been fraught with anxiety, not on their part, but from the airline staff. The computers weren't working properly so their bags had to be re-checked-in manually. The plane was late arriving due to an issue in Auckland, which had necessitated a change of aircraft. The normally relaxed and friendly Islanders were stressed and distracted.

Hehu, who was working at customs, came to say goodbye. They were relieved to see his smiling face. He said a prayer over them, praying for a safe journey and that they would find new beginnings in New Zealand. Jiao said "Amen", in agreement, she did hope for change, especially in her marriage situation and in her relationships with her children.

Jimmy had met her on the beach that morning for a final dawn walk. He too had prayed for her, saying he would never forget their time together. "Whatever happens, I will pray for you every morning" he had promised, "that you will walk closely with Father God and not stumble, that He will protect you and be your strength."

Jiao prayed for him, as the sea lapped over their feet. She prayed he would find a woman who would love him and be his companion, that their Father God would protect him and give him the desires of his heart.

She also thanked him that he had chosen to take her to church instead of his room, that he had chosen to bring her honour and friendship instead of shame and heartbreak. He said it had been a battle for him, but God had given him the strength to do the right thing. She told him she would always love him as a brother, and in her heart she knew that was now true.

Later he had come to the hotel foyer to wave goodbye as they boarded the airport shuttle bus once again. She didn't feel like the same woman who had uncertainly stepped off it only a few weeks earlier. Jimmy appeared after they were onboard, in his hotel tropical shirt uniform. He stood waving on the road. She saw a tear escape his eye, as they rounded the driveway airport bound.

Tanya was also working that day and though she had promised to do her best to make it to the airport, Jiao was surprised when she appeared, along with the children on the other side of the low wire fence that boarded the edge of the tarmac. The children jumped up and down waving their arms, shouting, "Aunty! Aunty! Lao Lao! Lao Lao!". Jiao waved and smiled at them, trying to suppress her rising sense of doom. For a moment, she seriously considered taking Wenling's hand and dragging her back the way they had come, but the poker-faced stewards were ushering them up the gangplank, so fighting all her instincts, she helped her mother embark.

Inside the plane felt dark and pokey. Ushered to the front row, they were directed to three seats with a screen wall in front of them. The check-in staff had explained that due to the change of aircraft, there was no business or premium class available, so they had been assigned the best seats they had, with close access to the toilet and a little extra foot room.

Jiao wasn't really worried about the luxuries of business class...the champagne, plump cushions or being able to lie back, the flight was less than four hours, but what she did feel glad about was being close to an exit! Some passengers had not got onto this flight and had been rescheduled for the following day. So, Jiao was thankful they had a seat. Although her heart tugged to stay, she knew it was time to return to the life she had left behind. She was glad too, that they had been allocated seats, as she didn't feel she could go through the emotions of saying goodbye again.

Jiao took the window seat, while Wenling huddled up next to her. The window looked old and opaque, so it was with difficulty that she squinted through it to catch a last glimpse of their newfound friends as the plane lurched into movement. An older man with an ornately carved stick was shown to the seat beside her Mother. They gave each other a nod, then he looked at his knees and Jiao wasn't sure if he was meditating or sleeping.

Take off was smooth enough, although noisier in a smaller plane. Wenling's hand, shaking sporadically, gripped Jiao's, she sat rigid with her eyes squeezed shut. Jiao sadly watched the blur of green and white that was the island, disappear behind them until there was only the bright blue of the sea. When they were airborne Wenling calmed a little, able to drink a glass of water and nibble a bag of nuts.

In front of them on the other side of the plane next to the door Jiao observed three young men chattering and laughing. One of them obviously liked the smiling stewardess who gave the safety brief and the other two were teasing him.

Jiao sighed, feeling a little foolish about her fears and took her newfound treasure out of her hand baggage: 'The Holy Bible'. Wenling was still trying to finish the romance she had been reading since their holiday began, opening it, she promptly fell asleep; the late night before and the delayed departure had obviously exhausted her enough to sleep, even in a plane!

Jiao asked for extra pillows and did her best to cushion her Mum into a comfortable position. The armrests between the seats wouldn't move, so she wedged her in at an awkward angle.

Jiao tried to read the words on the page, but her thoughts were distracted, her spirit restless. She closed the solid, new-smelling book and folded out the screen she found in her armrest. She tried to find something of interest to watch, but she couldn't focus, her heart was unsettled. Finally, she folded the screen away, leaned back her chair and closed her eyes.

For a moment she heard only the sounds of the hostess preparing coffee and tea, the strange hum of the pressurized cabin, but then the words of the song Tanya had written down for her, began to sing loud and clear her mind...

GOD WILL MAKE A WAY

God will make a way,

Where there seems to be no way.

He works in ways we cannot see,

He will make a way for me.

He will be my guide,

hold me closely to His side.

With love and strength for each new day,

He will make a way; he will make a way.

By a pathway in the wilderness, He'll lead me.

Rivers in the desert will I see.

Heaven and earth will fade,

But His love will still remain.

And He will do something new today.

Jiao felt a peace fill her. She heard the words Tanya had spoken about the Holy Spirit, *'He is with us, the Spirit of God, here on earth, our Guide, our Comforter, our Peace in times of trouble. We are never alone and don't need to be afraid'.* It was a strange concept, that God's Spirit had time to be with her.

Then she remembered the scripture Hehu had read aloud the night before:

> 'For who among men knows the thoughts
> of a man except the man's spirit
> within him? In the same way no one
> knows the thoughts of God except
> the Spirit of God.'

> 'We have not received the spirit of the
> world but the Spirit who is from God,
> that we may understand what God

Through her worldly eyes, it seemed to Jiao that God had given her nothing but heartbreak and disappointment, a husband who didn't love her, children who didn't care for her. But this peace she was feeling, told her something different.

She thought of Chaoxiang and could still feel a surge of resentment towards him for leaving their marital home, for not being a companion to her, for not saying goodbye.

The song words came back to her, 'By a roadway in the wilderness He'll lead me. Rivers in the desert will I see.' *Yes, Holy Spirit, my whole life seems like a wilderness, but show me the pathway. My marriage is like a dry desert; make a river run again. Bring Chaoxiang back to me and show me how to love him.*

Tea and coffee were served, Wenling slept on, so Jiao carefully drank a sweet black tea, then once the cups had been collected, she tried to sleep.

Jiao awoke to a lurch; the plane was rattling strangely. The pilot's voice spoke over the intercom, "This is your pilot speaking. Some ice has entered one of the engines, this is a common occurrence and not a cause for alarm." Jiao looked at her watch, they had been flying for less than three hours and still had an hour and twenty minutes to go. That meant they must be over the ocean.

Jiao's previous misgivings returned. There was a loud rattling and the pitch of the engine rose, then there was an audible "bang". Wenling grabbed the arm rests and let out a high-pitched moan. Jiao could hear gasps and cries from other passengers too. The high-spirited three boys in front, looked back, suddenly quiet and serious.

Behind her, she heard an anxious voice say, "Did you see that flash? Look the hostess is moving the passengers away from the wing where the flash came from." Wenling must have heard too; she began to panic, gripping Jiao's arm and breathing fast.

As the acrid smell of burning began to fill the cabin, Chaoxiang, Junjie and Lihwa's faces flashed before her mind. She felt thankful that she had written each one a letter, telling them she loved them and about their Heavenly Father. There was so much more to say, and she longed to hold them in her arms one more time but instead found herself silently praying for them. *Father God, please keep them safe, let them come to know about your love and find your Family, like I found it in these last weeks. Please let my Mum be with me in the place you have prepared. Thank you for finding me and for bringing me to the Island, thank you for the hope I have in you, even if this is the end.*

Wenling stared at her in horror, "How can you be so calm and happy?" She screeched, "We're going to die an awful death! This plane is going down!"

As she said this, the craft shuddered then began to fall. There was no more sound from the cockpit which remained firmly closed and the claustrophobic cabin filled with palpable fear.

Jiao took both her Mum's hands and held them in hers, "Look at me" she said. "Deep, slow breaths. It's going to be OK."

"You don't know that" Wenling spluttered back, "Why doesn't the pilot tell us what's happening?"

Just then the plane levelled again, then the high vibration stopped and there was an eerie echoey quietness to the engine's hum. Jiao fought a growing feeling of claustrophobia, it gave her the urge to run to the exit, to get out of this death trap. She could see the cockpit door and wanted to get up, hammer on it, and demand an explanation. She wanted to be able to tell her terrified Mother what was happening.

Pushing down these crazy thoughts she forced calm back into her voice and said softly, "If it is our time, at least we are together. I love you Mum. Thank you for always being there for me." She continued to hold her Mum's right hand in her left one. "And now I have felt His Love, I truly believe this will not be the end. Like Tanya read to us from the Holy Book...

'Jesus said, I am the resurrection and the
life. He who believes in me, though
he may die, he shall live.'

Wenling's body became less tense but a tear ran down her cheek as she whispered, "I want to believe Jiao, I really do." Then she closed her eyes and fell silent. Little did Jiao know that she was making a promise to God. A promise that should he bring her out of this alive, allow her to hold her grandchildren in her arms once more, she would follow Him faithfully for the rest of her days.

The pilot finally spoke again. "Due to an indication in the Flight Deck of a potential issue with one of the engines, we have shut down the left engine as a precautionary measure. We will begin a slow descent so please ensure your seats are upright, trays stowed, and seatbelts are fastened."

Wenling looked at Jiao with horror, "So now we've only got one engine!".

The old man beside them suddenly stirred and spoke in a slow but surprisingly audible and authoritative voice for a man with almost no teeth, " He is the Way, the Truth and the Life ...Yes, For God so loved the world that He gave His only begotten Son, that whoever believes in Him shall not perish, but have eternal life." He gave a wide gummy grin, stroked the large wooden cross that hung on a piece of leather from his neck, then laughing at Wenling's serious face said, "See you in Heaven Lady!"

A flight attendant appeared, a homely looking Maori lady in her 30's, she had kind smiling eyes and immediately recognized Wenling's signs of distress. "Don't worry" she said crouching in front of her, "These planes are designed to fly on one engine." She then gently returned Wenling's seat to an upright position, something Jiao had overlooked in the horror of the moment. "Do you need anything?" she asked, and Jiao guessed that she was a Mother herself, probably wondering if she would be arriving home to her own children that night.

"Water", gasped Wenling, obviously dehydrated after all her panicked panting. The hostess brought them both bottles of water and plastic cups. Jiao tried to help her Mum pour and drink the lukewarm water, as the plane lost altitude and began to sway precariously from side to side.

The ninety minutes that followed were interminable. No more news from the pilot, even their saintly hostess began to show the strain, though she continued to serve and re-assure as well as she could.

Jiao after initially seeing the foreboding dark ocean below, could now only see thick clouds and the ensuing darkness out of her window.

Nobody left their seats, but she could hear the loud wailing prayers of someone far behind them and noticed the young man with an eye for the hostess, had begun to shake uncontrollably. She also overheard the matter-of-fact voice of a woman nearby, who sounded like she had some aviation knowledge, "Oh yes, we'll be circling to use up any excess fuel. It's procedure before an emergency landing."

Jiao could hear the roar as the pilot eventually began to decelerate for the landing. The descent felt markedly steep and once again, Jiao wondered if they would survive or if the plane would burst into flames on impact. She muttered one final prayer, something Tanya often said, "Your will be done."

Kissed the side of Wenling's face, gave her hand one last squeeze, then closed her eyes.

They heard the bang of the landing gear locking in, they felt the bump as the wheels touched down, were violently shaken to the roar of the reverse thrusts, then the carriage slowed, the aircraft levelled and they came to a halt.

Passengers spontaneously began to cheer and clap in abandoned relief, Jiao and Wenling overcome with emotion both burst into tears.

Jiao wished the hostess could fling the doors open so they could breathe the outside air and see the ground, but instead she squinted out the window, where all she could see was a sea of fire engines and ambulances, flashing in the darkness.

When Jiao and Wenling were finally assisted down the ramp, Jiao was surprised how shaky her legs were and how hollow and strange she felt; numb with shock.

Part of her was disappointed that she was back in New Zealand, back to her sad and complicated life, that she hadn't 'gone home' to meet her Heavenly Father, that amazing presence of Love she had encountered in the church. That she hadn't got to see the 'Heaven' Believers sing triumphantly about. But she was also thankful that she was on solid ground and would see her earthly family again.

She thought of them and thought how different her homecoming would be to that of the lady returning to Rarotonga, who had been smothered with wreaths and embraces. Jiao didn't expect any greeting except maybe a merry salute from Chaoxiang's new driver ...if he was still waiting.

Wenling and their stick wielding travelling companion were both met by wheelchairs and promptly paired with an airport staff member. Around them the ambulances stood by, fire engines flashing. Jiao, still feeling a bit wobbly herself, walked between the two wheelchairs. Like herself, the old gentleman looked a little disappointed that He had not got the chance to meet his Father in Heaven, Jiao smiled at him and said, "Don't worry, our day will come." He smiled his gummy smile back at her and said, "I'm ready child!". Their eyes met and for a moment they connected in a way that reminded Jiao, that this funny man was her family too.

All the passengers were ushered to baggage collection, then guided to a large boardroom. They sat around the long table, were offered coffee and sweet tea, which Jiao and Wenling both gratefully received, followed by chocolate chip biscuits and cake in individual plastic wrappers. Wenling ate both but Jiao's stomach was growling for some real food. Maybe the driver could detour to her favourite Chinese restaurant for some dumplings and Dandan noodles ...comfort food.

The pilot, his co-pilot and the cabin crew entered the room. A round of applause arose from the passengers. The pilot, a male, looked little older than Junjie and his co-pilot, a female, looked even younger. They obviously weren't very experienced and Jiao was grateful that she hadn't seen them before the flight. The lovely flight attendant was now looking visibly shaken and a male flight attendant, who must have been in the back part of the plane, stood smiling a blank kind of smile, probably in shock too.

The pilot gave a short account of what happened, explaining that although the chance of engine failure was extremely low on these aircraft, they still underwent training three times a year in a simulator, so they had known the exact procedures to follow.

Some passengers asked questions, others wanted to thank the crew. One older lady was angry that there had been such a delay in information being relayed to the passengers, but the pilot levelly explained, that when the light had come on, indicating he had an issue with one of the engines, he had needed to follow a number of step-by-step procedures to shut it down. He explained his priority had been the safety of the passengers and crew and he'd given an update of the situation as soon as he was able to.

She was still unhappy, but the rest of the passengers called for another round of applause for the level-headedness and bravery of the pilot and crew. Jiao and Wenling clapped, Jiao was especially impressed by the hostess, who told them it had been her first flight back with the airline after taking a break to have children.

Debrief over, they wandered down a wide corridor, Wenling was pushed in the wheelchair and Jiao pushed the trolley loaded with their cases and hand baggage. They followed the other passengers towards customs and the exit. Jiao wondered if her own children had missed her at all. She wondered if Peng Sun, Chao's chauffeur had found out about their late arrival and waited, then she wondered if Chao had been upset by her letter and not sent a car to get them at all.

With rising anxiety, she arrived at customs, where they were rounded up once more and told by a member of the airline staff, that they would probably be approached by reporters but if they wanted to talk to them or not was their choice.

They were surprised as had it happened in China; they probably would have been told what to say.

Quickly passing through the checks and x rays with nothing to declare, Jiao walked towards the arrival gates, hoping with all her heart that Peng Sun would be there.

Sure enough, as the staff had forewarned, three reporters with large microphones in their hand's bee-lined towards them and the other passengers from their flight, but Jiao didn't have eyes for them. All she saw was the most beautiful picture. There, before her stood a crowd of familiar faces, in the middle was Chaoxiang with the largest bunch of red roses Jiao had ever seen, on one side of him stood Junjie, even taller now than his Dad, awkwardly holding a big heart-shaped box of chocolates, on the other side stood Lihwa, holding a pink foil balloon on a stick with 'I Love You' written on it. On either side of them, stood Fred and Lifen both smiling joyfully and to one side, a little apart from them, decked in his black and white suit and holding his cap in his hands, was Peng Sun, grinning a satisfied grin, as if all this was his doing.

Jiao felt as if she was in a dream, maybe they had crash-landed and gone to heaven, but as soon as Chao took her in his arms, holding her close like he had all those years ago, she knew it was real. He lifted her face gently holding them in his hands and looked her in the eyes, 'I'm sorry', he choked, 'I have never stopped loving you. Please give me another chance.'

A few minutes later, floating down the road in the back of Chao's favourite BMW, Jiao let out a sigh, her contentment more than she could contain Junjie sat in the front with Peng Sun directing him to Jiao's favourite restaurant. He had grown into a man, but looking back at her, his eyes were full of love and she knew she hadn't lost her 'little boy'. Wenling sat beside them, Junjie had brought a big fluffy pillow for her and she had promptly fallen asleep on it.

Behind them, were Fred and Lifen bumping along in Fred's green truck with Lihwa squeezed between them. They were laughing and talking animatedly. Jiao looked forward to the days to come, when she could share with each of them, all that had happened to her in her few short weeks on the Island.

But in the backseat of his car, Jiao relaxed fully, for what seemed like the first time in forever. Chaoxiang held her in his arms as if he would never let her go. Was it the letter or nearly losing her, she didn't know what had happened but she remembered the song's words...

'a pathway in the wilderness, a river in the desert'

...and she knew that God had made a way and He *had* done something new today.

THE END

EPILOGUE

A few words from the Author

I hope you enjoyed this, my first novella. You may also like to read my first publication, 'Finding Gold', a collection of poems and short stories, as well as an account of how I came to be a Believer or a 'Follower of the Way' as Christians were once known.

If you want to know more about the Heavenly Father that Jiao encountered in this story, I hope you too can find a local church or group of Believers that will welcome you into their family and share with you the good news.

Please be careful not to join a cult or any group preaching 'The Word of Faith', 'Prosperity' or 'Being Your Best Self' instead of the Gospel of Christ.

I say this because sadly, many 'Churches' worldwide are being transformed to the world, choosing to promise health, wealth and teaching self-help methods, instead of the teachings of Jesus Christ and the Word of God.

2 Timothy 4:3 (NLT) For a time is coming when people will no longer listen to

sound and wholesome teaching. They will follow their own desires and will look for teachers who will tell them whatever their itching ears want to hear.

1 John 4:1 (ESV)   Beloved, do not believe every spirit, but test the spirits to see whether they are from God, for many false prophets have gone out into the world.

Matthew 24:24 (ESV) For false christs and false prophets will arise and perform great signs and wonders, so as to lead astray, if possible, even the elect.

Colossians 2:8 (ESV) See to it that no one takes you captive by philosophy and empty deceit, according to human tradition, according to the elemental spirits of the world, and not according to Christ.

2 Peter 2:2--3 (NLT) .Many will follow their evil teaching and shameful immorality. And because of these teachers, the way of truth will be slandered. In their greed they will make up clever lies to get hold of your money. But God condemned them long ago, and their destruction will not be delayed.

Acts 20:28--32 (NLT) . "So guard yourselves and God's people. Feed and shepherd God's flock—his church, purchased with his own blood—over which the Holy Spirit has appointed you as leaders.[I know that false teachers, like vicious wolves, will come in among you after I leave, not sparing the flock. Even some men from your own group will rise up and distort the truth in order to draw a following. Watch out! Remember the three years I was with you—my constant watch and care over you night and day, and my many tears for you.

"And now I entrust you to God and the message of his grace that is able to build you up and give you an inheritance with all those he has set apart for himself."

There are many warnings to beware of false prophets and teachers and not be led astray in the New Testament, in fact it is one of the main recurrent themes. Today we see many established cults such as Jehovah's Witnesses, Seventh Day Adventists, Mormons, Catholics etc. that have added to or taken away from the Bible in order to create a different gospel to the one Jesus laid down his life to bring us.

There is also an emergence of TV and social media personalities, as well as people in mainstream churches, claiming to preach the gospel of Christ, but actually fulfilling these warnings, seeking self-gratification or financial gain.

This makes it all the more important to read the bible for ourselves so we can be sure that what we see and hear is the same gospel that Jesus Christ and the early church, lived and preached. The book of Acts is a good place to start, to learn about this, followed by Matthew, Mark, Luke & John. After that you can ask the Holy Spirit where to next or begin at the beginning with Genesis and the creation of the world.

In the Bible you will find everything you need for life ...business, family, romance, conflict, grief, trials... you name it, they are covered in the most holy and popular of books. There is nothing missing, nothing needs to be added. It is a book, but no ordinary book. This book is God-breathed and the more you read it the more it will speak to you.

It is a book of history, of knowledge and a book of prophecy. In it we can read the history of the world from beginning to end. We can also find mention of scientific knowledge long before discovery by human scientists, i.e.: the law of cause and effect, the importance of washing hands under running water, the laws of thermodynamics, the existence of light and radio waves, etc. if you are interested in this, watch 'Ten of the Top Scientific Facts in the Bible' on You Tube.

The Bible is also the greatest prophetic book ever written. It contains 735 predictions, of which at least 81% have already come true at the time of my writing this.

These are good reasons to read the Bible. Find a translation you like to read, also compare different versions. I love reading the New Living Translation, because it conveys both the word and the meaning of the original manuscripts, while also being poetic and easily understood.

If English isn't your first language, endeavour to find one in your mother tongue, as you read it, you will begin to understand what being a Christian means.

Because the Holy Spirit is here on earth, our helper, alive and well, able to live in us, He is able to speak to us as we read. Ask any Believer if the Bible speaks to them at different times, in different ways, even sometimes receiving the exact verse or message from different sources over a short period of time. If the Holy Spirit lives in them, they will tell you this is true.

This is what Jesus told his disciples...

> John 14:15-21 (NIV) "If you love me, keep
> my commands.

And I will ask the Father, and he will give
you another advocate to help you
and be with you forever—

the Spirit of truth. The world cannot
accept him because it neither sees
him nor knows him. But you know
him, for he lives with you and will
be in you.

I will not leave you as orphans; I will come
to you.

Before long, the world will not see me
anymore, but you will see me.
Because I live, you also will live.

On that day you will realize that I am in my
Father, and you are in me, and I am in
you.

Whoever has my commands and keeps
them is the one who loves me. The
one who loves me will be loved by
my Father, and I too will love them
and show myself to them."

Luke 11:11-13 (NLT) "You Fathers – if
your child asks for a fish, do you give
them a snake instead? Or if they ask
for an egg, do you give them a
scorpion? Of course not! So if you
sinful people know how to give good
gifts to your children, how much more
will your heavenly Father give the
Holy Spirit to those who ask him."

Later, when the people of Samaria heard Phillips message of
Good News about the Kingdom of God and Jesus Christ,
many were baptised in water. When the disciples in Jerusalem
heard they sent Peter and John to them.

Acts 8:15 (NLT) As soon as they arrived,
they prayed for these new believers
to receive the Holy Spirit.

Galatians 5:19-26 (NET) Now the works of
the flesh are obvious: sexual
immorality, impurity,
depravity, idolatry,
sorcery, hostilities, strife, jealousy,

outbursts of anger, selfish rivalries, dissensions, factions, envying, murder , drunkenness, carousing, and similar things. I am warning you, as I had warned you before: Those who practice such things will not inherit the kingdom of God!

But the fruit of the Spirit is love, joy, peace, patience, kindness, goodness, faithfulness gentleness, and self-control. Against such things there is no law. Now those who belong to Christ have crucified the flesh with its passions and desires. If we live by the Spirit, let us also behave in accordance with the Spirit. Let us not become conceited, provoking one another, being jealous of one another.

If you are new to the Bible, have been misguided by the many false teachings being preached or just want to study the Word of God afresh, I recommend watching the free online videos by www.bibleproject.com They explain the overarching story of the bible, books of the bible, the different types of writings, who is Jesus, who is the Holy Spirit, Heaven and Earth as well as lots of other concepts and books of the Bible in short, five-minute videos.

I also recommend listening to David Pawson. He was a wonderful Bible Scholar, who faithfully read and unpacked each book of the Bible in a deep but simple way. Most of his teachings are free to listen to online.

If you want to make an informed choice about becoming a Christian, you can read his booklets, including 'Explaining Salvation', 'Explaining the Key Steps to Becoming a Christian' and 'Explaining New Testament Baptism', all of which can be bought or downloaded for free from www.davidpawson.com

Another Bible based teacher I enjoy listening to online is Mike Winger. He teaches on many different topics and explains why some of the current 'Christian' teachings are not in agreement with biblical truth.

Romans 5: 1-5 (GNT) Now that we have been put right with God through faith, we have peace with God through our Lord Jesus Christ.

He has brought us by faith into this experience of God's grace, in which we now live. And so, we boast of the hope we have of sharing God's glory!

We also boast of our troubles, because we know that trouble produces endurance, endurance brings God's approval, and his approval creates hope.

This hope does not disappoint us, for God has poured out his love into our hearts by means of the Holy Spirit, who is God's gift to us.

James 1:12-18 (NET) Happy is the one who endures testing, because when he has proven to be genuine, he will receive the crown of life that God promised to those who love him. Let no one say when he is tempted, "I am tempted by God," for God cannot be tempted by evil, and he himself tempts no one. But each one is tempted when he is lured and enticed by his own desires. Then when desire conceives, it gives birth to sin, and when sin is full grown, it gives birth to death. Do not be led astray, my dear brothers and sisters. All generous giving and every perfect gift is from above, coming down from the Father of lights, with whom there is no variation or the slightest hint of change. By his sovereign plan he gave us birth through the message of truth, that we would be a kind of first fruits of all he created.

Being a Christian does not mean all our problems go away or life will be easy. In fact, when we read the library of sixty-six books which make up the Bible, we read of lives filled with every sorrow, conflict, relationship issue, illness, persecution, injustice etc.. that we could ever expect to encounter.

Most people know that the course of life does not always run smoothly. This is the same for Christians. In fact, the very stance of being a Believer or standing up for the truths and principles found in the Bible, can itself lead to persecution, ridicule, or even being disowned by friends and family.

Maybe this was one of Jesus' underlying messages in the scripture Wenling was confused by...

> Mark 12:46-50 (NLT) As Jesus was speaking to the crowd, his mother and brothers stood outside, asking to speak to him. Someone told Jesus, "Your mother and your brothers are standing outside, and they want to speak to you."
>
> Jesus asked, "Who is my mother? Who are my brothers?" Then he pointed to his disciples and said, "Look, these are my mother and brothers. Anyone who does the will of my Father in heaven is my brother and sister and mother!"

Jesus also said...

Mark 13:12-13 (NLT) "A brother will betray his brother to death, a father will betray his own child, and children will rebel against their parents and cause them to be killed. And everyone will hate you because you are my followers. But the one who endures to the end will be saved.

So, there is no promise that we will not suffer if we become followers of Christ but the promise is, that if we can keep the faith until the end, our death or His return, we will be saved and receive eternal life in the New Kingdom and New Earth to come.

In the last book of the Bible, it is written:

Revelation 20:4 (NET) Then I saw thrones, and seated on them were those to whom the authority to judge was committed. Also I saw the souls of those who had been beheaded for the testimony of Jesus and for the word of God, and those who had not

worshiped the beast or its image and
had not received its mark on their
foreheads or their hands. They came
to life and reigned with Christ for a
thousand years.

I will conclude with Jesus's words to His Disciples and one of my favourite Bible verses. I hope you too, become a Disciple of Jesus and like Jiao that you experience first-hand our Father God's love.

I hope you can find a church or group of friends, that will embrace you, love, support and encourage you as family, the way the Bible calls us to as fellow Believers. I also look forward to meeting you one day, in our Father's House...

John 14:1-3 (ESV)

Let not your hearts be troubled. Believe in
God; believe also in me. In my
Father's house are many rooms. If it
were not so would I have told you
that I go to prepare a place for
you? And if I go and prepare a place
for you, I will come again and will

take you to myself, that where I am
you may be also.

ISLE OF HOPE

ISLE OF HOPE

Lightning Source UK Ltd.
Milton Keynes UK
UKHW021536220321
380783UK00008B/1425